NICK & CO. on Holiday

When Nick & Co. go camping it's a riot from start to finish. The gang's arrival certainly livens up the sleepy little country village of Tidesbourne. And before long Nick & Co. find themselves in the middle of an adventure. What is Old Tom's secret?
And who are the mysterious sheep-stealers?
Nick & Co. are on the trail again.

This is the second book about Nick & Co. Their first adventure, *Nick & Co. in a Fix*, is also published by Lion Publishing.

Bob Croson, the author, is married to Jean, an artist, and they have two teenage sons, Bill and Ben. His hobbies are playing golf, writing stories and relaxing after gardening. He is also headteacher of a community junior school in Derbyshire.

NICK & CO
on holiday

BOB CROSON

A LION PAPERBACK
Tring • Batavia • Sydney

Copyright © 1987 Bob Croson

Published by
Lion Publishing plc
Icknield Way, Tring, Herts, England
ISBN 0 7459 1346 6
Albatross Books Pty Ltd
PO Box 320, Sutherland, NSW 2232, Australia
ISBN 0 86760 906 0

First edition 1987

British Library Cataloguing in Publication Data

Croson, Bob
    Nick and Co on holiday. —— (A Lion
    story).
    I. Title
    823'.914 [J]   PZ7
    ISBN 0-7459-1346-6

Printed and bound in Great Britain
by Cox and Wyman, Reading

CONTENTS

1

A BIT OF BOTHER

Church Street wasn't the best cricket pitch in the world, but in my imagination it was smoother and flatter than any Test Match wicket I had seen on TV.

My best pal Sparky passed me the ball, and I paced back from the lamppost, striding into the distance trying to look mean and hard. I turned and looked round. The batsman was waiting impatiently.

'Oh come on, Nick, get on with it!' she said. It was Sparky's sister, Sam. She was really good at most sports, which was a bit maddening at times. Both Sam and Sparky played in school teams for all sorts of things and were very athletic and quick.

I looked at the rest of the gang to check if they were all in the right places. Sparky was standing ready for a catch, and Raj was looking very correct behind the wicket, made from an old cardboard box. He was ace at cricket and dead keen to play for England when he grew up.

But the rest!

Whizzer was leaning on a lamppost, clicking his fingers to the rhythm coming from his headphones. Chip — a computer-freak — was bent over his latest game. And as for Franco Granelli

— Lump to friend and enemy alike — he was, as usual, eating!

That only left my pesky little sister Mo, who was busy holding on to Wally, our dog, who didn't understand the rules of cricket!

I didn't bother shouting at them all. It wasn't worth the effort. Besides, I thought I could get Sam out easily and they wouldn't be needed.

'Botham races in, one ball to go, one wicket to take. Will he win it for England yet again?'

I raced in and bowled as hard as I could. The tennis ball sped in Sam's direction and, 'WHAM!' She socked the ball high in the air.

'Get it,' I yelled.

Now I didn't mean Wally, but the ever-obedient if slightly stupid dog didn't understand. Hearing his master's voice, he wrenched himself free of Mo and hurtled off after the ball.

Lump never moved, Chip didn't notice and Whizzer clicked his fingers in time to the music only he could hear, with a blank smile on his face.

'Mine,' I yelled as I sped off after the ball.

'Mine,' yelled Sparky as he did the same.

'Come back, Wally,' Mo shouted as she chased after our daft dog.

Now, it would have been a brilliant catch if it hadn't been for Mr Marchbank. He was a very correct, retired teacher. You could set your watch by him. He always bought sausages on a Tuesday at exactly the same time from Mr Blake's butcher's shop on the corner of Church Street, opposite our youth club. It was also right on the boundary of our pitch. Just at the moment he stepped out of the shop, Sparky and I arrived to catch the ball, closely followed by Wally.

There was a terrific 'CRUNCH!' as we all collided. Mr Marchbank fell to the ground, his sausages beside him. Sparky and I lay in a tangled heap at his feet.

The ball bounced off the bald top of Mr Marchbank's head, and with great skill Wally leaped in the air and caught it. He brought it to me in his mouth, his tail wagging wildly.

Then Wally saw the sausages. The prize for all his hard work! He dropped the ball and grabbed them.

'No!' yelled Mr Marchbank.

'Leave!' I screamed at Wally.

His tail drooped, he dropped the sausages and skulked off to Mo, wondering what he had done wrong.

I picked up the sausages, dusted them off and sort of pushed them back into shape, smoothing over the dog bites, wrapped them in what was left of the paper, and handed them back to Mr Marchbank. He did look a funny colour. Sort of purply-red!

'Are you all right, Mr Marchbank?' I asked politely.

It was like watching a kettle come to the boil. Suddenly the steam came out.

'You blithering, idiotic, wicked children,' he shouted angrily. He was obviously struggling for words.

We just stood there, feeling rather uncomfortable. And it was a relief to see Doug arriving on the scene. He is our youth club leader, and is brilliant at rescuing us from scrapes.

Doug raced over to pick Mr Marchbank up, helped by Mr Blake the butcher.

'They should have taken my advice and closed down that blessed youth club, it's nothing but a nuisance,' Mr Marchbank complained.

That made me see red. When I thought of all we'd done to keep our youth club! But I kept my mouth shut.

'Are you all right?' Doug asked, ignoring the outburst. 'I'm sure the boys didn't do it on purpose. It was a very unfortunate accident. When the new playing-field at the back of the club is finished this sort of thing won't happen.'

'And none too soon,' Mr Marchbank grumbled.

'Now,' Doug went on, 'those sausages are beyond repair. Mr Blake, will you give Mr Marchbank some more and add a couple of those lovely chops you have in the window? I'll pay now and the gang will pay me back later.'

We all looked at each other, horrified. I got little enough pocket-money as it was, without keeping 'Old Grumblechops' in breakfasts!

'Right you are,' Mr Blake said and went into the shop.

'Bang goes my new cricket bat,' I muttered grimly.

'Anyway,' Doug cut in sharply, giving me a sidelong glare, 'as I'm taking this lot off camping for a week, you'll have some peace, and by the time we're back, the playing-field should be ready.'

'Thank goodness for that,' Mr Marchbank grunted and disappeared back into the shop to collect his goodies.

'Right, you lot,' ordered Doug. 'Into the hut. Quick march!'

We all trooped into the club hut, with Wally following, wagging his tail. Dumb dog!

'At least I got you out,' I said to Sam, as we flopped down on the chairs.

'You never,' Sam complained. 'It was a six!'

'No way. Wally caught you, off Mr Marchbank's head.'

Wally wagged his tail in agreement.

'He doesn't count!' Sam said, angrily.

'Hang on, hang on,' Doug cut in. 'It's not important. And before you leave I want contributions for the sausages.'

'Wait a bit,' Lump complained. 'I wasn't playing.'

'Guilty by association,' Doug replied. 'And I haven't got time to argue.' As well as being our club leader, Doug was also the curate of our local church, a sort of trainee vicar. But if you think religious people are just softies, you should meet Doug. He can be tough, but he's always fair.

When I first got to know him, he really got on my nerves, going on about Jesus and God and things, but after a while I began to realize what he was on about. He actually did all the things he talked about. Actions speak louder than words, they say.

Through him and Sparky, most of us had become regulars at Doug's club meeting after Friday games nights. That was when Doug would tell us stories from the Bible and make them really come alive. I used to think they were dead boring. But with Doug they made a lot of sense. He really made me change my mind about God and Jesus,

11

and take being a Christian seriously.

'Before you lot all slope off,' Doug went on, 'I want some help in packing up things for the camp.'

'I'll do the food,' Lump chipped in, quick as a flash.

'No, you won't,' Sam said. 'We want some left.' Lump's parents owned the local chip shop and the whole family was, shall we say, keen on food.

After a bit of arguing about who did what, we helped Doug pack the camping gear which we had borrowed from the local scout troop, as well as the food. We were off to Tidesbourne the next day, Doug's home village, and his mum and dad would be getting some of the equipment to save us transporting it in the hired van.

It was the first time any of the gang had been camping, and I noticed Doug was looking rather nervous.

'Right, you lot,' he said, 'be back here, tomorrow morning, nine o'clock sharp. And don't be late.'

The next morning dawned bright and clear — just the day for a holiday. I said goodbye to Wally — and waved to Mum and Dad — and set off for the church hall. Little Mo had already gone to call for Sam.

The van was the oldest and most beaten up vehicle I have ever seen. In my humble opinion it should have been cut up into little pieces and used for making tin cans years ago, but Doug insisted it was perfectly all right. Anyway, it was all we could afford.

After we had packed our gear and sleeping-bags, Doug called us together for a final chat.

'Now look,' he started, 'this holiday has been paid for as a reward for all that you did last year to help the police catch those car thieves.'

We all glowed with pride as we thought back to the excitement of last year (though there were *some* incidents which I'd rather forget).*

'Now, this time,' he went on, 'we are going on a holiday. Right?'

'Yes, Doug,' we replied.

'And we are not looking for any adventures.'

'No, Doug.'

'And we certainly don't want to get involved in anything dangerous, do we?'

'No, Doug.'

There was a long silence.

'I'm telling you this because there has been a bit of bother recently in the village,' Doug said. 'But we're not going to get involved. We're there to have a holiday. Right?'

'Yes, Doug,' replied Chip and Lump.

'Cowards!' I grunted at them. Then I asked Doug, 'What trouble?'

'Never you mind,' Doug replied. 'I'm just telling you to keep your nose out! We are on holiday and not getting involved. Right?'

'You know me, Doug!' I responded, with a twinkle in my eye, nudging Sparky.

There was a pause. I leaned back in my seat, looked up at the ceiling and spoke, to no one in particular:

'Nick and Co., righters of wrongs, modern-

---

* See *Nick and Co. in a Fix* for the gang's first adventure.

day Robin Hoods, England's answer to the A-Team . . .'

I was suddenly bombarded with cushions from all sides.

Doug just held his head in his hands and groaned.

I just couldn't wait to get there!

2

RUN FOR IT!

'Old Macdonald had a farm,
Ee-i-ee-i-o.
And on that farm he had a four-eyed, one-legged,
flat-nosed, green-eared,
duck-billed platypus, and his dog, Spot,
what a lot,
Ee-i-ee-i-o.'

The van trundled through the Derbyshire countryside, with us singing to relieve the boredom.

I was sitting between Sparky and Raj. Opposite us sat Whizzer, Lump and Chip, and piled all round our feet were all the bags and junk. Mo and Sam were sitting up front with Doug.

'Only a mile or two to go now,' said Doug cheerily, joining in with the chorus.

'BANG!'

Suddenly the organized tangle of bags jumped up and hit me in the face, Lump bounced podgily to the floor, and the rest of us lurched around all over the place.

'Hold on!' Doug called out.

'That's great,' I thought. 'He says hold on, when it's like being inside mum's washing-machine!'

Then I was thrown on top of Lump who groaned loudly as the wind was knocked out of him.

'Good job he's so fat,' I thought, grateful for the soft landing. We skidded to a stop and Doug turned round to see if we were all right.

'Everyone OK back there?' he asked.

There was a muffled and painful groan from underneath me and the pile of cases. My comfortable landing-mat had now become an erupting volcano as Lump surfaced from the bottom of the van growling, 'Gerroff!'

Doug came round and opened the back of the van and we all fell out, a pile of bags and bodies. We were in the country, by a wood.

'Wh-what happened?' asked Whizzer, pulling his earphones off. How he managed to keep listening to Reggae music through all the chaos I'll never know.

'Sorry, fellas,' Doug apologized. 'We had a puncture — a front tyre — and I nearly lost it.'

'I don't think you ever found it,' I grumbled.

For some reason Doug didn't seem to like this remark. I can never understand why adults get so touchy about their driving. My dad becomes a raving lunatic behind a wheel, especially when he sees a woman driver. But you tell him if he does anything wrong and he goes berserk!

'I don't think your driving is getting any better,' added Sam.

'No, it's always been terrible,' said Little Mo rubbing her bruised shoulder.

'Where are my sandwiches?' complained Lump, digging around for the 'snack' he'd been eating.

We all fell about laughing, because it was obvious to everybody else exactly where Lump's sandwiches were. He must have landed on them and now they were stuck very firmly to the back of his jeans!

He groaned and began the messy business of scraping them off, while we stood watching Doug trying to change the wheel of the van.

'You're not very good at it, are you?' put in Chip, knowingly.

Doug just turned and looked at him. 'Why don't you go away and have a wander round while I sort this out?' he asked through gritted teeth.

'Come on,' said Sparky, 'let's have a game of hide-and-seek.'

It was better than sitting around getting bored, so I agreed.

'Last one to the tree's on!' I shouted as I made a dash to the nearest one.

The others hurtled after me, all except Whizzer, who had been fiddling with his headphones. When he realized what was happening he was so far behind us he couldn't even beat Lump to the tree. So we left Whizzer to count to a hundred while we all dashed off in different directions, leaving Doug to deal with the wheel in peace.

I ran as fast as I could for a narrow lane which branched off the main road. The trees leaned over, making it like a dark tunnel, and I looked around for somewhere to hide. The undergrowth was thick with nettles. Suddenly I saw the back of an old lorry parked by the side of the lane ahead of me. It had a tarpaulin cover, and I jumped up on to it, looking for a place to hide. It smelled horrible, piled up with dirty, smelly sacking. I jumped down quickly, holding my nose, and ran into the clearing behind it. In the gloom of the wood I could see an old caravan. It looked disused. The curtains were closed.

I could hear someone coming down the lane, so I hid round the back of the caravan. From my hiding-place I saw Lump approaching, red-faced and looking for somewhere to hide. He looked around and then ran over to a large tree and tried to hide behind it. No way! Sticking out one side I could see a mop of black hair and on the other a large backside, still carrying the remains of the squashed sandwiches.

I almost laughed out loud, but that would have given me away, so I just clamped my hand over my mouth and held on tight. I crouched behind the caravan for what seemed an age. In the distance I could hear faint sounds of laughing and shouting.

Eventually, along came Whizzer.

It was funny watching him creeping round the lorry and into the clearing, trying not to make a sound, crouching down and then standing on tiptoe, looking for us.

In the end, he resorted to cheating.

'One, two, three. Nick, I see you,' he shouted.

But I wasn't fooled — he was looking in the other direction.

Then Lump erupted from behind the tree. A wasp, attracted to the sandwich remains, had been buzzing around him. Suddenly it attacked Lump with a well-aimed sting!

'OWCH, OW, GERROFF!' screamed Lump, holding his backside, and leaping into the clearing.

At the same moment the door of the caravan burst open and a man came storming out. He was wearing a pair of greasy, stained trousers and a dirty shirt. His angry, stubbly face jutted out as he looked round to see where all the noise was coming from.

Whizzer was rooted to the spot in surprise. But Lump couldn't stay still because of the sharp pain in a certain tender part of his anatomy. The man grabbed Whizzer's arm, dragging him over to Lump, who was imitating a Red Indian war dance.

'What're you two doing here?' he bellowed angrily. 'This is private land. You're spying, aren't you! Sid, Sid, get out here and give me a hand,' he called in the direction of the caravan.

I watched in horror from behind the caravan. I had to do something to help. But what? I didn't think walking out and explaining that we were only playing hide-and-seek would really work.

'Who sent you here?' the man went on, looking very nasty.

There was nothing for it; I had to do something quick and drastic. I jumped out from behind the caravan, making as much noise as I possibly could. I pushed the man over, and Whizzer broke free.

'Whizzer, Lump, run for it!' I yelled. We all dashed round the side of the lorry and into the lane. It took the man by surprise and gave us a head start on him and Sid. But Lump was having difficulty in running and holding his wasp-sting at the same time and he tripped and fell over, groaning and complaining. Whizzer and I hauled him up, totally ignoring his complaints, and dragged him on down the lane. I could hear the men shouting behind us.

'Get your fat frame going,' I shouted. 'Or we'll all be caught.'

'I'm trying, I'm trying,' he replied breathlessly. 'But I am in pain, you know,' he said.

'Come on, man, come on,' urged Whizzer. Together we dragged Lump along the lane. What a weight! But we did it, and before long we burst out onto the main road.

The van was all ready to go, and the rest of the gang were already inside, waiting for us.

'What on earth's the matter?' asked Doug, as he saw us arrive.

'Don't ask, I'll tell you later,' I replied breathlessly.

We heaved the complaining Lump into the back of the van and Doug started it up.

As we set off, I looked out of the back window to see the men running out onto the road, and shaking their fists at us . . .

'What on earth was that all about? You haven't been up to something you shouldn't, have you?' asked Doug.

'Oh, it was nothing,' I replied. 'A misunderstanding.'

I didn't think it would do any good to explain. Anyway, Doug might want to go back and talk to those men and I for one didn't think that was a good idea.

We weren't far from the village — and I just hoped we wouldn't come across those two again.

But I had a feeling in my bones that it wasn't the last we had seen of them!

3

IN AT THE DEEP END

It was very quiet in the van. Well, we were quiet, but the van sounded as if it was shaking itself to bits.

'Look, there it is!' Doug said, as we came over the crest of the hill. The village of Tidesbourne was below us, nestling in a wide green valley dotted with farms. Beneath the heather-topped hills, we could see the village, a higgledy-piggledy tumble of houses.

'Cor, isn't it pretty? Like an advert on the telly,' Sam said.

Even Whizzer had switched off his Walkman and was looking out of the windows with the rest of us, admiring the view. When we reached the village we drove past old stone cottages and gardens packed with flowers. In the middle of the village was some grass and a pond with ducks. A bit further on we turned into a gateway and drove down a tree-lined drive.

'Hey Doug, do you live here?' Chip asked.

'I used to,' Doug replied. 'You know where I live now — it's only just down the street from you.'

'Come down in the world, haven't you?' inquired Lump. 'What did you do wrong?'

'I didn't do anything wrong,' replied Doug. 'I

wanted to work in the city.'

'You must be stark raving mad,' Whizzer said.

Before the conversation could continue, we skidded to a halt on the gravel drive in front of a big house.

'Right, everybody out,' Doug called.

This time we climbed out very slowly. It was very grand and I had great difficulty stopping my mouth dropping open.

The door opened, and out stepped a grey-haired lady in a tweed skirt.

'Douglas, where have you been? We were quite worried about you,' she said, putting her arms round Doug. She gave him a hug and a kiss. It was funny seeing your youth club leader and church curate being treated like a little boy by his mum. I could tell Doug wasn't that keen and made a mental note to tease him later.

'Hello, Mum,' he replied sheepishly.

We all looked at each other and sniggered.

'I hope she's not going to try that game on me,' I thought, and edged behind the others.

She turned towards us and I could feel everyone leaning towards me, trying to get as far away as possible from the chance of a sloppy kiss.

'These must be our guests,' she went on with a smile.

We all smiled nervously back. I could feel that knotted tingly feeling you get in your stomach when you are not sure what's going to happen next.

She reminded me of an aunty of my mum's who visited once a year. I looked forward to it the same as I looked forward to a visit to the dentist.

Every year it was the same. When she arrived it was like being enveloped by a huge, lavender-smelling duvet, and when you surfaced from that there was a walloping, sloppy kiss. Ugh!

Doug introduced us one by one, and I decided on a distant 'Hello' from behind the protection of the rest of the gang. Thankfully she didn't try to kiss any of us.

'By the way,' she said to Doug after greeting us, 'it's our annual garden party in aid of the Old Folks Home today. I thought you wouldn't mind joining in.'

Doug turned and looked at us, then back at his mum. She didn't give him a chance to argue.

'Come on in, children,' she said brightly, ignoring Doug. 'Leave your bags in the van, I'll show you where the bathroom is, then you can join us. It's only a buffet.'

'What do we need a bath for?' Lump whispered in my ear. 'Does she think we smell?'

'No, you wally,' I whispered back through my teeth. 'She's telling us where the loos are.'

Mo looked confused. 'What's a buffet? What does it taste like?' she asked.

'It doesn't *taste* like anything,' Sam replied. 'It's what you have at a wedding.'

Mo looked puzzled. 'Are we going to a wedding?' she asked.

Doug butted in. 'Don't worry, Mo. You're not going to a wedding. What Sam means is that the food's on a table, so you can help yourself. It's like that at a lot of weddings.'

The talk of food spurred everyone to action. We followed Doug into the hall and waited while

Whizzer tried out the bathroom. Soon he came bounding down the stairs.

'Hey man,' he gasped, shaking his head, 'that bathroom's incredible, fantastic. It's like something in a film.'

After that we all had to try it! It was *huge* — with gold taps, and plants and a deep-pile carpet.

Eventually we were all ready and made our way into the garden through some large glass doors. In front of us was an enormous lawn with tables of food and groups of grown-ups standing around.

It all went quiet. The gang huddled behind me. We didn't like being looked at. I stuck my hands in my pockets and tried to look relaxed, but inside I just wished I was home.

A man came up.

'Hello, everyone,' he said. 'I'm Doug's father. Come and have something to eat.' He had a kind face — just like Doug's.

We followed him down to the tables. Some people smiled and said, 'Hello', and I began to feel a bit better.

As we reached the food our eyes lit up. There was a fantastic spread of sandwiches and cakes. Lump looked ready to eat the tables as well!

Nobody moved until I picked up a plate and carefully placed a sandwich on it. Suddenly, as if that was some sort of signal, the rest of the gang all lurched forward after the food. The sandwich was knocked from my plate and I was pinned against the table.

'Back,' I hissed through clenched teeth.

'Sorry,' muttered an apologetic Lump, trying to clean bits of bread off me with his hands. I pushed him off and stepped back. The gang descended on the food like at the school Christmas party. I could see people looking at us, so I grabbed Sparky's arm.

'Calm them down,' I muttered. 'Everybody's looking at us. We're making real fools of ourselves.'

But before long everyone had piled food onto their plates and sat down on the grass to eat. I wandered round the garden, smiling at a few people and saying hello, trying to look as if I went to this sort of thing every week. Then some of the gang followed me about, staring at things and pointing.

'Cor, look at that swing in the tree.'

'Ain't there a lot of flowers, it's like a park.'

'Hey, look at all those goldfish in that pond.'

Eventually the girls got up and wandered over to talk to somebody by the house and Lump set off towards the table in search of more food. The others joined me and we walked over to the swimming-pool.

Raj and Chip ran off to the deep end to inspect the diving-board. Sparky and I stood by the side trying to work out who had got the most swimming certificates. Whizzer, behind us, was listening to his Walkman; I guess he was nervous and didn't want to talk to anybody.

As Sparky and I talked — well, argued — I could see Lump wandering back with the biggest piece of cake you've ever seen. It was topped with two sorts of ice cream. Lump was obviously looking forward to it. His eyes were fixed on the cake and he walked straight into a rosebush. I nudged Sparky and pointed, laughing as Lump picked his way out of the roses. His concentration restored, he headed our way.

I suppose I should have thought quicker, and remembered that Lump loses all functioning brainpower when focusing on food. Too late I realized that Whizzer, with his back to Lump and the Walkman on full blast, couldn't see or hear Lump approaching.

'Watch out!' I yelled.

Almost in slow motion, Lump barged into the back of Whizzer, who fell towards me, knocking me backwards into the pool. I felt the warm water close over my head, then surfaced, just in time to see Lump's huge bulk landing in the water right on top of me. He had slipped on the ice cream spilt in the collision.

Once more I went under and started to thrash about. Eventually I remembered it was the shallow end and stood up!

Lump was still spluttering and yelling, 'I'm drowning, I'm drowning,' when I grabbed his collar and made him stand up too.

'Sorry, Nick,' he muttered, sheepishly.

I could feel the anger rising up inside me. What was worse, there was a crowd of grown-ups standing around laughing. I didn't think it was funny. I had half a mind to climb out of the pool and punch somebody on the nose.

Doug rushed over. He took one look at my face and, with Sparky's help, got us both out of the pool and into the house, away from everybody.

27

They tried to calm me down as I dried off. Somebody brought our bags from the van.

'Huh, what's up with everybody,' I grunted as I rubbed a towel through my hair, 'laughing at me like that.'

'Oh, come on,' said Doug. 'It was funny.'

'Lump won't think so when I get hold of him,' I cut in.

Lump cowered in a corner.

'That's not fair,' Sparky went on. 'It was an accident.'

'Yeh, like the accident of my fist-accidentally-catching his nose!' I said.

I was really mad — steaming!

Eventually, after I had been left alone for a bit, I calmed down and started thinking straight again.

It was a bad start to the holiday. Over the last few months I'd been trying what Doug calls 'self-control', and asking God to help me. Just when I thought I'd learned how to stop losing my temper so easily, there it went again!

Carefully keeping our distance, Lump and I joined the rest outside.

It was time for us to leave and set up camp. We said our goodbyes and made for the van.

'Right, dear,' Doug's mum said to him, 'the rest of the things you need have been put under a tarpaulin in the field you'll be camping in. We've put up a couple of large tents and a toilet and a kitchen tent. All you have to do is put up the tents for sleeping. Mr Staples, the farmer, said there should be no problems — just to keep away from the animals and machines. With all the trouble he's been having he is a bit edgy, but it shouldn't affect your camp!'

My ears pricked up at the mention of trouble. I wished someone would tell us what it was all about.

We soon reached the campsite and set about putting up our four tents — not something we did every day. We were hopeless. There were tents, pegs, ropes, and other assorted bits and bobs everywhere. It was hysterical! Sparky and I made a good team. I held up the tent by standing inside it while Sparky banged in the pegs. But I couldn't resist making ghost noises at Mo, and frightened her to death. Unfortunately, at this point I collapsed, laughing, with the tent all about me.

Doug was not amused. In the end he had to put it up by himself, with us 'helping' — in between attacks of hysterical laughter which left us in a heap on the ground.

Doug sent me and Sparky to collect water from the tap in the corner of the field while Whizzer and Chip fetched wood from Mr Staples' farm to make a campfire. Good old Doug! While we put down our sleeping-bags and sorted ourselves out, he made cocoa on the camping-stove and we had some of his mum's fruitcake. It's funny how everything tastes better out of doors.

While we were sitting around the campfire, I suddenly remembered something said earlier in the day.

'Doug?'

'Yes,' he replied suspiciously.

'What is it,' I went on, 'that's been happening, that you don't want us to get involved in?'

He sighed. 'You really don't need to know,' he

said. 'It's nothing to do with you.'

I wasn't letting him off that easily.

'But if we don't know what it is,' I continued, 'we might get involved with it before we know we shouldn't!' The others all murmured in agreement.

At this point, Doug gave in.

'OK,' he said, 'I'll obviously have no peace till I tell you. Mr Staples has been having terrible trouble with a gang of sheep thieves. The police don't seem to be able to catch them and there are all sorts of rumours about who is involved and why they are doing it.'

'Is that all?' Whizzer complained. 'I thought it was something serious.'

'It is,' Doug continued. 'To city folk it doesn't sound a big deal, but to people around here it is very serious. If these people aren't stopped or caught, Mr Staples could easily go out of business.'

'Hmmm,' I said, my mind going ten to the dozen. 'Where do we start?'

'By going to bed,' Doug said flatly.

Eventually, we settled down in our tents. I was with Sparky and Chip. Sparky's been my best friend since we started school. It was difficult getting to sleep, and Sparky and I kept on thinking up jokes — until Doug told us to shut up. It wasn't exactly comfortable, sleeping in a tent. But, after wrestling with my sleeping-bag for hours, I gradually drifted off to sleep.

Suddenly, there was a terrific CRASH!!

Waking in an instant, I was ready for action.

'The sheep thieves,' I yelled. 'Let's get 'em!'

4

SHEEP THIEVES!

Leaping out of my sleeping-bag and diving out of the tent, I yelled for everyone to wake up. Almost immediately, Whizzer, Sparky, Sam, Raj and Mo were by my side. Lump never stirred, and Chip was still trying to get out of his sleeping-bag.

Doug sleepily emerged from his tent.

'What's going on?' he groaned.

'We're under attack. Didn't you hear the noise?' I hissed at him. 'I reckon it's those sheep thieves!'

'Good grief!' he muttered.

'Look!' Sam shouted. 'Over there!'

It was a clear, moonlit night, and in the eerie glow we could see the canvas of the kitchen tent moving.

There was someone inside!

Doug looked alarmed.

He picked up a piece of wood by the campfire and told us all to stand quite still. Slowly he crept over to the tent and pulled back the flap.

'Come out, whoever you are,' he demanded.

The tent moved again, but no one came out. So Doug decided to go in. There was silence for a moment, suddenly broken by Doug's voice.

'What on earth?' he yelled. Then even louder, 'Get out of here!'

There was a tremendous racket from inside the

tent, with pans and boxes falling everywhere. Before we could make up our minds whether to run for it or jump in to help, two dark shapes leaped out of the tent, quickly followed by Doug.

With sudden relief, we all fell about laughing.

'Baaa,' the shapes complained as they scurried off into the night. It was two sheep, upset that their suppertime snack had been interrupted.

'Right, everyone, back to bed,' Doug said, sounding relieved. 'We'll sort the mess out in the morning.'

We woke up next morning feeling cold and stiff — and rather tired. But after our first breakfast, cooked by Doug, Chip, Raj and Mo, with only minor burning of the sausages and the merest sprinkling of grass on the bacon, we all felt better and set about tidying up.

Sam and I were on washing-up duty. She soon got me organized. My mum says I've got a 'soft spot' for Sam. She's not bad, I suppose, and, as she's Sparky's sister, I've known her for a very long time. I mean, I'm not keen on girls — but Sam's OK. Most of the time. I wasn't looking forward to doing the cooking. It was something that Mum always does in our house and is a complete mystery to me.

It was a good job that people in the village had invited us out for meals, and Mrs Staples, the farmer's wife, was making packed lunches for us every day.

In fact, the next thing we were going to do was visit the farm and say hello. Our field was by a stream some distance from the farm itself. We had to cross a couple of fields and go round the edge of a wood to get there. Perhaps it was just as well they couldn't see the field from the farm.

The farmyard was surrounded on all sides by buildings, and Mr and Mrs Staples were in the farmhouse kitchen. Doug had warned us that Mr Staples could be a bit stern and we were to mind our tongues. He was a big man, who didn't seem to smile much. His wife looked totally the opposite — small and jolly with twinkling eyes.

'Good morning, everyone,' Mr Staples said solemnly. 'Welcome to Staples Farm.' We all stood there quietly, rather frightened of him. I hardly heard what he was saying but I did hear him tell us he would let us have a good look round the farm that morning, but that he would appreciate it if we kept as much as possible to the field we were camping in.

'I haven't got time to show you round, so I'll send along one of the men,' he concluded, and marched off.

'Don't mind him,' Mrs Staples said, looking at our glum faces. 'His bark is worse than his bite. And he's got things on his mind. The sheep thieves, you know.'

'Is it that serious?' Doug asked.

'Why, yes m'dear,' she replied. 'If it goes on like this we could lose the farm before the winter.'

This really was something for Nick and Co., I thought to myself.

'But anyway,' she went on, 'you're here on holiday and nothing must spoil that. When you're ready, your lunches are on the kitchen table. Oh, and here comes Bill to show you round.'

33

A very brown and weathered, tough-looking man came over.

'Hello there,' he said. 'I'm Bill Groves, Bill to you lot. Shall we go?'

Leaving Mrs Staples, we followed Bill on a tour of the farm. After showing us the barns and machines, he took us to see the animals.

He showed us where the cows were milked, and a barn where some new calves were being kept with their mother. The calves were lovely — they sucked my fingers and nuzzled against me. It was the first time I'd ever really *touched* a farm animal. Next we looked at the hens that Mrs Staples kept. They were 'free-range' — just walking about the farmyard. Then Bill pointed to a large building a little way off.

'Let's go to the pig unit,' he said, and we trooped after him.

In one part of the unit were narrow stalls with lights hanging over them. In two of these pens were enormous pigs and rows of little piglets fighting for their mother's milk.

'Lots of lovely bacon,' Lump commented, smacking his lips.

It quite put me off breakfasts. While everybody was 'ooing and aahing' at the piglets, I wandered out to have a look round.

Round the other side of the building were larger pens with little houses at the back. Some were filled with pigs, but one or two were empty. I wandered into one of these empty pens to have a look round. But meanwhile Bill, still inside the building, had moved everyone on and was just about to open the inside door of the pen, not knowing I was there. Before I knew what was happening, what seemed like hundreds of pigs came screeching out at me.

I leaped into the air and as I landed the pigs started nipping at my ankles. An immediate strategic withdrawal was called for. Heading for the nearest wall, I vaulted it with a skill that could probably have taken me into the next Olympics.

In the Olympics, the high jump has a comfortable landing area; unfortunately my choice of landing was a rather large pile of muck. I landed well and truly in it. It smelt terrible — and so did I!

By now, the others had appeared. When they saw me, they just collapsed with laughter. I stood up, and with all the dignity I could muster, stormed off. Inside I was screaming with anger and embarrassment.

I made off along a farm track down one edge of a field. Running as hard as I could helped me to calm down a bit. When I was totally out of breath I had to stop. By then I had reached the wood that we'd passed on our way to the farmhouse. Bending down to wipe some of the muck from my trousers, I suddenly noticed something moving in the wood.

It didn't look like an animal. Could it be someone up to no good? A sheep thief? I walked on slowly and then turned quickly to face the trees. This time I definitely saw a pair of eyes looking back at me before they disappeared. Was this a chance for Nick Baker, single-handed, to catch the sheep thieves? Forgetting Doug's advice, and without thinking about what might happen, I decided attack was the best form of defence.

I suddenly turned and leaped into the wood. A dark shadow flitted away through the trees and I hurtled into the undergrowth in pursuit. Suddenly I burst out into a clearing and grabbed my quarry round the ankles. He fell, and I sat on him.

'Ouch,' he shouted. 'Gerroff.'

I was pushed off and a boy about my age ran across the clearing to where two other people were standing, looking at me in disbelief.

'Good grief,' I thought. 'What have I got myself into now?'

They stood there — a boy and a girl, both with bright ginger hair, and an old man.

'He's mad,' the boy said to the others, pointing in my direction.

The old man, who had a kind, reassuring face, looked across at me.

'Are you all right?' he asked.

'Yes,' I replied cautiously. Then I turned to the boy. 'Why were you watching me?' I asked.

'Why were you running like a lunatic?' he replied. 'And why do you stink so much?'

'Why don't you mind your own business?' I barked back.

'Who are you anyway?' he said.

'Hold on, hold on,' cut in the old man. 'This isn't getting us anywhere.'

'Ginger,' he said to the boy, 'that's not the way to talk to people.'

Then he turned to me. 'Don't mind Ginger,' he said quickly. 'He thought you might be up to no good.'

'A sheep thief, you mean?' I replied, looking quizzically at them.

He didn't answer. Instead, he told me who he was. His name was Tom Marsh, and he lived in the smallholding next to Staples farm, the boundary of which went right through the middle of the wood. The two kids, Ginger and Mave, were his grandchildren. Tom also told me that Mr Staples wanted the wood cleared, but that he was against it because it contained so much wild life.

'Lots of people think it's me taking the sheep,' he went on. 'But it isn't.'

Before I could ask him about it we were interrupted.

'What's going on here then?' came a loud and very stern voice.

5

MORE MYSTERIES

The voice startled both of us. I turned to see Mr Staples standing there, looking very angry.

'Marsh,' he said, 'I thought I told you to keep off my land.'

'We were in "our" part of the wood,' replied Tom, 'when Ginger here heard something suspicious.'

'Huh,' Mr Staples grunted, then he turned to me. 'I thought I told you not to go wandering. Get back to the others,' he said angrily.

I was just about to object when he said, 'Now!' in a voice that I didn't dare disobey. Tom and his grandchildren went off in the other direction.

'Keep away from them, boy,' Mr Staples said as we set off back to the farm. 'They're a bad lot, always involved in bother. I'm sure it's them taking the sheep, but he's so fly the law haven't managed to get him yet. But I will!'

I was going to argue, but decided not to. Mr Staples didn't look in the mood to discuss anything.

When I got back to the farm nobody wanted to come near me. They all held their noses and Doug said, 'Nick Baker. How *do* you do it?'

Mrs Staples was kind and helped me get cleaned up. When I went outside again I was introduced to Frank, who also worked on the farm. He was much younger than Bill, and a very friendly sort of guy.

While I was in the farmhouse, I had overheard Frank telling Mr Staples that some more sheep had been rustled sometime during the night. Mr Staples had said he was going to set the law on old Tom Marsh, as it must have been him.

We were standing outside, wondering what was going to happen next. Looking at Mr Staples, Doug decided to cut short our farm tour, and we gathered up our sandwiches and trooped back to the campsite.

On the way back, Sparky had a go at me.

'What are you playing at?' he complained. 'You're already in bother and it's only day one.'

I told him all about Tom and about what I had overheard, but he was unimpressed. Sometimes Sparky really gets on my nerves, especially when he's right! I knew that as usual I was beginning to go over the top and get carried away.

We had a really good afternoon playing cricket. Then it was my turn to help cook. Trust me to get the grotty jobs! First I had to peel the spuds, millions of them, and then help Doug cook a strange mixture that he called hot-pot. While we were stirring it like two old witches, he had a word with me.

'About earlier,' he began.

'I know, I know . . .' I interrupted. 'There's no need to go on.'

I could do without being told where I was going wrong on the very first day of the holiday.

Seeing he was going to get nowhere, Doug left

me to stir the horrible brew, making a comment as he left about me being good at stirring. I didn't like that.

My mind drifted away during this boring occupation, and I was dreaming about how, one day, I would have a house like Doug's parents, with a swimming-pool. I would sit in the garden, stirring my drink, and listening to the sounds of birds calling.

'Nick!'

It wasn't a bird calling, it was Sam yelling at me.

Coming out of my daydream, I realized that the delicious cool drink I was stirring was a horrible hot-pot, and the revolting brew was bubbling over the side of the pot and spilling on to the cooker.

Sam turned off the gas, and then turned on me.

'What are you playing at, and where's Doug?' she demanded.

'I don't know, and I don't know,' I replied grumpily. 'And anyway, this is a woman's job!'

I shouldn't have said that. You should have seen Sam's face!

'How dare you!' she blasted back. 'I suppose you think that all a woman should do is shut up, wash the clothes, cook the food, and do anything else that her lord and master commands her.'

'Well I . . .' I began to reply.

Fortunately, Doug came back and rescued me.

'Come on, you two,' he said. 'Save your arguments, there are more important problems to deal with!' He pointed to the burnt mess in the pan. Sam flatly refused to help, so Doug and I had to open some more cans of beans!

After the meal we had what Doug called a

'camp time'. We had a sing-song, a few games, and finished with a talk from Doug before bed-time. He talked about Jesus and how he forgave people — even the ones who condemned him to death, when he had done nothing wrong. We talked about how God could help *us* to forgive other people.

That started me thinking. It's a whole lot easier to be thankful when God forgives, than to forgive other people when they say sorry for the things they've done to me!

I thought about how I felt about Lump at the pool, and Mr Staples. Forgiving people was easier said than done!!

Just then Sam came up to me and apologized for losing her temper with me. That really hurt, because I knew I was the one who should have done the apologizing. I mumbled something back but I felt terrible inside.

'Time for bed,' shouted Doug. 'And don't for-get to clean your teeth.'

'Grown-ups!' I muttered, beneath my breath. But I managed to get into my sleeping-bag with-out Doug noticing I hadn't been near a tooth-brush.

The following day, Sunday, we went to church. It was OK. In the afternoon it poured, and a 'kind' lady asked us to go to a concert in the village hall. It was an old wooden building, a bit like our old club hut. I hoped the concert would be good fun, but it was boring — very, very boring! Most of it was a choir of old ladies singing old-fashioned songs. I suppose they were doing their best, but before long, my mind began to wander. At least we weren't out in the pouring rain.

Looking round at the others, I could see they were bored as well. Whizzer was listening to his music with an earphone under one hand. Sparky, Sam and the others just sat there — bored out of their skulls.

Then it was time for a poetry reading by the village postmistress, a very — shall I say, large? — lady.

I glanced across at Lump.

Disaster!

He was gently nodding off, having eaten too much lunch. I just knew what would happen next!

Sure enough, after a little while, a noise like sawing wood came from his direction — the dreaded Granelli snore. You couldn't take him anywhere! He had gently fallen over onto Chip's shoulder, who gave him a fierce jab in the ribs. This woke him up with a start — not a good idea with Lump.

'Whoa . . .' Lump groaned loudly, at the same time as lashing out with his arm, knocking Chip to the floor.

The resulting commotion stopped the show. The local District Nurse, sitting only a couple of rows away, was convinced that Lump had had a heart attack. Poor Lump came very close to being given the kiss of life by this formidable lady. Yeeuuch! Just in time, he managed to convince her he was all right.

After that little incident the show carried on — worse luck! I gave Lump one of my withering 'Don't you dare do that again' looks, but all he did was smile stupidly back.

At last, it was the end! We clapped wearily. What a relief! It had also stopped raining and the sun was shining. We all rushed out to the village green.

I sat with Sam and Sparky on a bench, tossing stones into the pond.

Suddenly I noticed Old Tom, Ginger, and Mave cycling along towards us. I waved to them, and they stopped.

'Hi,' I said, but before I could get talking to them Ginger interrupted.

'Let's go, Granddad,' he said.

'I think it's better that we go,' Tom said. 'There'll be another time.' And with that they were off down the road.

'What was all that about? Who were they?' Sam asked.

I told Sam and Sparky the little I knew about Old Tom and his grandchildren. I didn't know *why* they'd been in such a hurry, though.

Then I saw the reason. As I looked back to the hall I saw the local policeman wandering round the side of the church, pushing his bike. He just smiled at us and set off up the road — in the opposite direction to Old Tom, Ginger, and Mave.

We got up and went to find out where Doug and the others were. I heard the noise of something coming along the road behind us. Looking over my shoulder I saw an old lorry stop by the village green. Turning round, I could see two people in the cab, but couldn't make out what they looked like.

There was something about the lorry that made

me curious, and I started to walk back towards it. However, before I could get anywhere near, it roared off at speed down the road. I turned back, deep in thought.

Just at that moment there was a screech of brakes. We all ran towards the noise. Tom was lying in the road with Ginger and Mave kneeling over him. Their bikes were scattered round, and the lorry was nowhere to be seen.

'What happened?' I asked breathlessly as we arrived on the scene. Tom was just coming round.

'That stupid lorry came hurtling down here at a stupid speed, and we had to throw ourselves out of the stupid way!' Ginger shouted.

Tom began to struggle to his feet.

'Are you all right?' Mave asked, helping him.

'Yes,' he replied. 'Just winded.'

'I'll go and get the policeman, he can't have gone far on that bike of his,' Sparky said in his usual efficient way.

'No, it's all right, no harm done, no need to get the police, they only make a fuss,' Tom insisted.

Tom, Ginger, and Mave picked up their bikes, and without another word, set off.

Why didn't they call the police? And why were they in such a hurry to get away? Strange!

I looked down the road in the direction the lorry had gone, to see the three cyclists disappearing into the distance.

'There's something fishy going on here!' I said out loud.

'Oh no,' groaned Chip. 'No more adventures, please. Let's just have a quiet holiday.'

6

THE CHURCH STREET CHASERS

'By the way,' Chip continued, taking my mind off the mystery of the crashed bikes, 'what about the races tomorrow. You haven't forgotten, have you?'

I had! The next day was the Tidesbourne annual village sports and we had persuaded Doug to let us enter as a team. We'd show 'em! We'd take on the kids from local villages. After all, we'd been practising for weeks. Doug had said I was taking the whole thing too seriously, but I wasn't having anybody laughing at us and calling us weak townies. We'd spent ages choosing our team's name. I suggested 'Nick's Army' — it had a sort of ring to it, I thought, but I was out-voted! We eventually agreed on 'Church Street Chasers' — Sam's idea — not bad, I suppose. It looked good on our banner. Sam flatly refused to wear a short skirt and prance around as our cheer-leader — I thought she would have looked rather good — but we did think up a great chant:

> 'Church Street Chasers are the best,
> Church Street Chasers'll beat the rest.
> Run and race as hard as you might.
> We'll still beat you out of sight.'

'You *have* forgotten,' said Chip accusingly.

Thankfully Whizzer joined in. 'Yeah,' he interrupted, 'I've been looking forward to it, man. All the practice has made us into finely-tuned machines ready for anything!' He flexed his muscles, then turned and pointed up the road. 'I mean, look at Lump!' he said.

I looked in the direction Whizzer was pointing.

'Grief,' I groaned to everyone. 'What chance do we stand with him? It's not that Lump's fat particularly, he's so dumb with it.'

'That's a bit mean,' cut in Sparky. 'You shouldn't talk about him like that, and he's not so dumb.'

I just looked at Sparky and raised my eyebrows.

'OK,' Sparky went on, 'he may make the odd mistake, but don't we all?'

I hadn't got time to argue, I had to fix my mind on the competition ahead, so we decided to get together the next morning for a final practice.

The practice was absolutely hopeless. This time I was determined not to lose my cool, but only just succeeded. The field where we were camping wasn't exactly right for running, what with long grass and hidden humps and hollows. Added to that, nobody was taking it seriously, and the more I went on, the more daft they became. I thought we should just practise running, catching and jumping but even that seemed to much for them.

Raj and Whizzer kept hiding in the long grass and popping up suddenly making daft noises. Sam and Sparky got a giggling fit and couldn't even stand up! Chip wouldn't concentrate at all, and kept drifting off to play with an electronic game he had brought. Little Mo tried hard, but her legs were so short that she couldn't keep up with the rest of them. And as for Lump — well, what can you say! It wasn't that he was so big, but you would think that a bigger person had more brain cells. Not in this case!

I dreaded to think how we'd do!

It was a lovely day and there was lots to do and watch at the sports. There were sideshows and stalls, and everyone was enjoying themselves so much that I threatened our team with terrible tortures if they didn't turn up on time for the races. I killed time by trying out various sideshows, and won a couple of coconuts, which I passed on to Doug for that night's tea.

As it got close to the start time we made our way to the sports-field. There were six teams in the competition — ours, one from Tidesbourne village, and four from neighbouring villages.

The first event was the egg and spoon race. We had put Chip into it because he was the technical sort. What a mistake! He might be good at pressing buttons and connecting circuits, but asking him simply to balance an egg on a spoon was something else.

He set off all right, but twenty metres down the track he tripped over his own feet and the wooden egg went rolling off in another direction.

'Pick it up, you dimbo, and keep going!' I screamed at him from the side of the track.

Obediently he ferreted around until he found it, replaced it on his spoon, and chased after the rest. Fortunately some of the others had similar difficulties and he managed to finish third. He was pleased. I wasn't.

'A blind bat with a wooden leg could have done better,' I grunted.

'Oh Nick, you're not starting again,' groaned Sparky beside me. Sparky didn't have time to hang about for my response because he was in the next race. He is the niftiest and quickest sack-racer I know, so I was quite confident there would be nobody to beat him. There was a lad from the village who was also in the race, and I heard him telling anyone who would listen about how he would easily win this race.

'Not this time, sunshine,' I said quietly under my breath.

The starter lined them up and I could see the village lad slyly looking across at Sparky. The gun went off and first they had to get into their sacks. It was here that the lad pulled his stunt. While he was getting in he leaned over, pretending to slip, and knocked Sparky over.

'Eh, ref, come on,' I yelled to the starter, but he took no notice.

I began to get worked up, but thankfully Sparky was more cool-headed. He leapt back to his feet and dived into the sack. The others were off down the track, and it was a while before he caught up with them, leaping along like a kangaroo with its tail on fire. There was no way that he could catch the leader, but then pride got the better of Tidesbourne's sack specialist.

What he did was very understandable, but all the same it was very foolish. He made the big mistake of looking round, admiring the cheers of the crowd and seeing just how far he was ahead.

'Arrgghh!' he yelled as his foot caught in the sack and he fell full length, just two metres from the winning tape. Quick as a flash, Sparky was past him, and had won.

Pride really did come before a fall! The lad was so miffed that he threw his sack down and stormed off without even crossing the line to get a point. I would never do a thing like that!

Next came Little Mo in the obstacle race. She couldn't run very fast, but was so nippy through all the hoops and nets that she came in a very honourable third. I was very pleased with my little sister, and didn't even rise to Sam's comments about girls being able to do just as well as boys.

I was dreading the next event. One of the rules was that everybody in a team had to do something. Now it was Lump's turn. We had chosen the potato race, because it was the shortest distance to run. He had to throw three potatoes into a bucket. Surely he couldn't muck that up?

The gun went off and Lump, under pain of death, put everything he'd got into it. He set off down the track like an Olympic sprinter — well, sort of! He lurched to a stop at the first potato, picked it up, and carried on to throw it in the bucket. Then he turned, ran for the second potato, grabbed it, and set off back to the bucket again.

Unfortunately, success went to his head and he turned to wave at the rest of us watching him. This spoilt his concentration and, as he passed the third potato, he trod on it, reducing it to a squidgy pulp. Only he didn't notice.

Triumphantly he threw the second potato in the bucket, then turned to look for the last one. His face dropped as he realized what he had done, saw the 'mashed' potato, and heard the laughter of the spectators. Even I felt a bit sorry for him. He looked confused, then decided to carry on. Much to everyone's amusement he set about picking up the bits of potato. Unfortunately, in doing it, his ample bulk strayed into the next lane, where another lad was coming along.

The effect was like a snooker shot. The lad bounced off Lump and into another racer, who lurched across the path of the guy in the end lane. Lump meanwhile cannoned off, and into the path of the remaining two competitors, who tried to take avoiding action and ran into each other. There were potatoes, buckets, and bodies everywhere.

It was so funny.

I laughed so much I was nearly sick.

The race had to be declared a draw, which was a better result than I had expected, so I was quite pleased.

The last event in the team competition was the relay, and we had to win it to claim the team trophy. We had saved our strongest team: Sam, Whizzer, Raj, and myself. We would win it easily, of that I was sure. In fact, I felt supremely confident. The village teams looked easily beatable and in Raj we had a county standard runner.

It was a complicated race. The first two runners did a hundred metres each, the next runner did two hundred, and the last four hundred.

Sam and Whizzer would take the first two legs,

Raj the third, and me the fourth, which wasn't run in lanes.

At the gun, Sam set off and kept a reasonable position; Whizzer then took over and pulled us into the lead with a fantastic run. Then Raj built up an even bigger lead — until the last twenty metres, when he pulled a muscle. In spite of the pain he struggled on to pass the baton to me. One of the village lads had already warned me to be careful of one of the boys I was racing against. He was called 'Grabber', and was determined to win, however he did it.

As I waited for Raj to reach me with the baton, Grabber pushed me out of the way to get the inside track. After taking the baton I set off in pursuit of the leaders, having fallen back into fourth place. I quickly made up the gap and slotted into second place, behind Grabber. He looked over his shoulder at me and sneered. Along the back straight, away from the crowd, he began to slow down till we were all bunched up tight, but when I tried to get past he speeded up again. What was he playing at?

Suddenly he slowed down again, this time catching me off guard. His foot hit my leg and knocked me off balance, and I fell to the ground. The lad who was third fell in a heap on top of me and we were left to sort ourselves out while Grabber raced away to victory.

I complained loud and long about what happened, but no one would listen. And, to make matters worse, Grabber's team won the cup.

'There ain't no justice,' I growled, and stormed off.

7

LUMP GOES MISSING

I got away from the crowds and sat down grumpily. I started pulling up tufts of grass and thinking of all the nasty things I could do to that swine Grabber.

'Come on, Nick,' said a voice. It was Sparky.

'Shut up,' I replied quickly. 'Don't start lecturing me, and don't give me a sermon.' And I added as an afterthought, 'If you do, I'll punch you on the nose.'

He sat down beside me and never said a word.

Slowly the boiling mood inside me calmed down, and I began to think straighter.

'All right now?' Sparky asked.

I grunted.

'You've done it again, haven't you?' Sparky said.

'What?' I growled.

'Completely lost your head. You always do it, and it never works!'

'Hmm,' I responded. He was right as usual.

Sometimes I could cheerfully strangle him, but I couldn't do without him. Like all real friends, he was always there to help when he was needed, however badly I treated him. And he often had the right thing to say. Not that I always listened straight away!

'Remember what Jesus said about forgiving,' Sparky went on. 'Even people who treat you rotten, like that lad on the track.'

I grudgingly admitted he was right.

It wasn't easy, but I began to feel better. I would try to forgive Grabber, but I still wished he hadn't won the last race.

'Worse thing is, there's no one to stop Grabber in the sprint now Raj is injured,' I grumbled.

We had no answers.

I looked across at the sports field and noticed three familiar figures watching events from outside the fence.

One of the village lads who was walking past noticed them as well.

'It's a pity . . .' he said. 'But he wouldn't.'

'Who are you talking about?' asked Sparky.

'Ginger over there,' he replied, pointing. 'He's the fastest runner I know, but he won't race.'

'Why?' I grunted.

The lad just shrugged his shoulders and walked on.

We just had to win the sprint! Not being able to think of any other idea apart from hitting Grabber, I decided to try persuading Ginger to join us.

'Wait here,' I said to Sparky.

I wandered over to where they were standing, trying to think of what to say.

'Hello,' I greeted them.

Ginger and Mave said nothing.

'Hello,' Old Tom replied. I noticed he was sporting a black eye.

'How'd you get that eye?' I asked.

'Oh, it just happened, must have walked into

the door,' replied Tom.

But at the same time Ginger added, 'Got it when he fell off his bike!'

I looked at them and wondered what on earth they were trying to hide.

'What do you want?' Ginger asked aggressively.

'Oh, someone says you're a very fast runner,' I replied. 'And I wondered if you would like to enter the last race.'

'No,' was all he said in reply.

I guess that would have been the end of it if Grabber himself hadn't come along.

'Nasty eye you got there,' he said to Old Tom, with a wicked grin on his face.

'Why you . . .' Ginger said as he lunged out at Grabber.

Tom pulled him away, but Grabber just laughed and walked off.

Then I had an idea.

Turning to Ginger I said, 'You don't like him, do you?' Not waiting for a reply I carried on, 'Bet you'd like to find some way of beating him! Now, my pal who was to race against him is hurt, but if you entered the last race you could take his place and beat Grabber out of sight.'

'No!' put in Old Tom quickly.

'Yes,' contradicted Ginger, still obviously fuming from Grabber's comments. Before he could be stopped he jumped the fence and followed me over to the others. We fixed it up with the race organizers and then made our way to the start.

Grabber was looking evil.

The gun went off on this last, special 200 metre

sprint for the individual prize. Ginger was off like a rabbit from a trap, and was miles ahead before the rest even got going. He didn't need any protection from me! There was no way anyone could get near him, and he had already finished before the others were halfway down the final straight. He stood with his hands on his hips watching the rest struggle to the finish.

'I'll . . . get . . . you . . . for . . . this . . .' gasped Grabber.

Ginger just turned and walked back to Tom and Mave. He didn't even wait for his prize.

I leaned on the fence, watching them go, and tried to work out what on earth was going on in this village. I hadn't cracked it yet, but super-sleuth Nick had never been beaten — yet!

The day after the sports, Doug organized a hike. Before we came away he had made a hike sound great fun, a spectacular adventure.

I should have known better! Grown-ups are brilliant at making things sound fantastic. You know the sort of thing. 'Oh, by the way, Nick, tomorrow we are going to see Uncle Arthur. You won't be bored, he's great fun.' Uncle Arthur is ninety, and can't stand children. Last time we went I took my remote control car to liven things up and he nearly had a heart attack when I drove it between his feet.

Right from the start, things went wrong. The lovely weather of the weekend had changed to a cloudy, misty and very grey day. I had geared myself up in an old, thick sweater, school anorak, old jeans, football socks and trainers. The rest of the gang looked equally bizarre in a strange selection of gear.

Chip looked really miserable. 'I don't want to go,' he moaned. 'I'm cold. If God wanted us to climb mountains, why has he made it so difficult?' All he wanted to do was to play with his computer games.

We hadn't named him Chip because he liked a certain food that goes with salt and vinegar. It was because of his crazy passion for computers. His family came from the West Indies and his dad was a teacher at our school. They encouraged him. As far as I was concerned, computers were only useful for playing occasional games on. The rest left me cold, especially when we did it at school. But for Chip computers were his life — much more exciting than going up one hill and down the other.

'I'm not The Grand Old Duke of York, and don't want to be,' he went on. 'All we'll do when we get to the top is come down again. Waste of time!'

As for Lump — he was whining louder than my dog Wally when he got a thorn in his foot. He wasn't keen at all.

'What are we doing this for anyway?' moaned Lump. 'It's cold. Wouldn't it be better if we left it for another day? Or year?'

'Oh, do stop moaning,' Doug said as he hustled us along through the village. 'You'll enjoy it.'

I goose-stepped behind him and said in a German accent, 'Ve haf vays of making you valk!'

Doug didn't like that.

The others did!

Sam laughed so much she nearly fell in the pond.

'Come on, you lot,' Doug bustled, 'or we'll be late.'

Doug led us to an old house just outside the village. There was a sign outside saying, 'Outdoor Pursuit Centre'. It was run by two men who looked about nine feet high. I decided straight away not to be cheeky to them! I think the others felt the same. They were called Joe and Dougal. Looking across at Sam, I could see her going weak at the knees. Pathetic!

'Gather round,' Joe ordered us, and we dutifully stood and listened. 'Inside,' he went on, 'we have kit for anyone who needs it. We will check out what you have and supply anything extra. I think we should be able to kit all of you up.'

I could see him looking a bit dubiously at Lump.

We were taken inside and shown racks of clothing and boots, and set about getting ready. Sparky pulled on a pair of boots and did an impression of Charlie Chaplin. Then he put on an enormous cagoule and a woollen balaclava hat and did his Donald Duck voice. What a hoot!

Meanwhile Lump was struggling to find suitable gear. If the trousers and cagoules were big enough round the waist, they were far too long. If they were the right length, then everything was too tight. Whizzer suggested a shoehorn or a pot of vaseline. But eventually Lump found something to fit.

We all gathered together at the entrance again. Sam was already there, swooning around the two instructors. Honestly! A few muscles, a stubbly chin, and she breaks into the 'You Tarzan, Me Jane' routine. You know, all fluttering eyelashes and the old, 'Aren't you wonderful' looks.

Sparky looked at my face as we went out. 'Careful, Nick,' he said, with a twinkle in his eye. 'Someone might think you're jealous.'

I trod on his foot hard, and he yelped with pain.

We had only gone a mile or so when it started to drizzle. After another mile the drizzle turned to rain, and then we climbed into the damp and soggy mist.

Lump dragged along at the back, looking totally miserable. I could hear Dougal encouraging then bullying him, trying to keep him up with the rest of us. Poor old Lump, it really wasn't his day.

At last, we reached the top of the peak — to find it wasn't a peak at all. What a con! It was an enormous, smelly peat bog. The mist was very grey, and the ground very black. It looked more like something from a horror movie than the top of a hill in the Peak District.

We stopped for a break and Sparky and I dropped into a gully to share a bar of chocolate.

'You enjoying your holiday?' I asked Sparky.

'If you mean right this minute, not a lot,' replied Sparky. 'If you mean all together, yea, it's cool. What about you?'

' 'S'alright,' I responded. 'Mind you, some of the things that happen are a bit odd, like disappearing sheep, and people behaving mysteriously.'

'Don't you think you're exaggerating a bit?' he asked.

I ignored this and went on, 'Look at the way

Old Tom is treated. It's not right, it's odd.'

'Mr Staples was saying that Tom and his family had been in trouble with the police before,' Sparky added.

'Your trouble is . . .' I started to reply, getting a bit cross. But I was interrupted.

'Gather round, everybody,' Doug called urgently.

When we looked out from the gully we got a shock. The mist had come down and you could hardly see your hand in front of your face. We clustered together, a grey and bedraggled group of figures.

'Here's another fine mess you got me into,' I muttered at Doug.

'Don't worry,' Doug said with a worried look on his face.

'Right,' Joe said. 'Rather than go on with the weather closing in, we're going to turn back and go straight down the way we came.'

Chip started to sing 'The Grand Old Duke of York' sarcastically, but stopped when he saw Doug's face.

'Listen carefully,' Joe went on. 'I want you to walk in line, staying within sight of the one in front. If you do lose sight, I want you to shout out loud and clear and we will all stop. Don't talk to anybody and lose concentration. If you do as you're told there will be no problems at all. I will go in front and Dougal will be at the back.'

I thought he was going a bit over the top, but he was bigger than me, much bigger, so I didn't argue.

It was wet and misty, really grotty, and nobody ·

looked happy. What a lovely way to spend a holiday! Tired, wet, and fed up, we made our way back to the village.

It was horrible, not knowing where we were going. None of us would admit to being scared, and when we got back we all made a great show of how clever we had been. I guess by the time school started in the autumn the story would sound like the first ascent of Everest, but all we wanted to do at that moment was get out of our wet clothes.

'Er, Doug,' Chip said suddenly. 'Have you noticed anything?'

'What do you mean?'

'Where's Lump?'

Lump was nowhere to be seen. We called and called but there was no response.

Where had that stupid idiot got to now?

8

NICK BLOWS HIS TOP

There are days when Lump drives me right up the wall.

There are days when he just irritates me.

There *are* times — a few — when he is actually useful.

But if ever there was a prize for being a pain in the neck, Lump gets the gold medal!

Joe and Dougal decided to call out the mountain rescue team and, as we stood at the entrance to the Centre waiting for them to arrive, I could only think badly of Lump. I wasn't so much worried about him being lost, just angry at all the inconvenience he was causing.

'I do hope he is all right,' Sparky said.

That made me even more angry, because I knew I ought to feel like that, too.

'He's just a stupid pain,' I replied sharply, angry at both him and myself. Just then a landrover screeched to a halt and several people got out. It was the mountain rescue team who had been on a training exercise nearby.

Joe turned to us.

'Who was behind him on the way down?' he asked. Timidly, Chip stepped forward.

'I was,' he admitted. 'And Nick was in front of him. But I swear that I never lost sight of Lump in front of me, unless I . . . I . . . er . . . mistook Lump for Nick.'

'You what!' I exploded. 'There's no way I could be mistaken for that fat freak, especially from behind!'

I turned away in disgust.

Doug then turned his attention to Chip.

'Are you *sure* of what you are saying?' he demanded. 'If you had paid more attention, we might not have been in this mess. Honestly, you lot are about as reliable as . . . as . . . my old van!'

If he hadn't been so angry, I would have laughed.

Chip looked crestfallen. 'I can't understand it,' he muttered.

Joe turned to Chip. 'Don't worry,' he said. 'It could happen to anyone. We'll find him all right.' And with that the rescuers, including Joe and Dougal, got into the vehicle and set off in the direction of the hills.

Doug turned again to Chip. 'I'm sorry,' he said. 'I guess I got carried away and didn't think. I shouldn't have gone on at you like that.'

Then to us all he said, 'I think it would be good if we all prayed that Lump will be found safely.'

Every time we get in a pickle, Doug suggests we pray. It's not that I don't believe in God, because I do. It's not even that I don't believe that praying, talking to God, works, because I do — I've seen it work. It's just that it's very embarrassing standing around in public and talking to someone you can't see. People might think you're mad!

However, at Doug's insistence, we asked God

to look after Lump and bring him back safely. Then we all set off back to the camp to wait. On the way Sparky walked with me as I grumbled along, kicking a stone.

As we got to the centre of the village, I noticed Ginger and Mave sitting by the village pond looking at the ducks. I wandered over, forgetting Lump for a bit, once more intrigued to find out what was going on.

'Hello again,' I said.

'Huh,' Ginger replied.

Mave looked at me and forced a half-smile.

I had been thinking a lot about how they fitted into the mystery, and why they didn't seem to have any parents, just Old Tom.

'Er, Ginger,' I asked. 'I was wondering. Why haven't we seen your parents about?'

Both Ginger and Mave looked sharply at me.

'What's it got to do with you?' Ginger grunted aggressively. Then, changing the subject, 'What are you doing here anyway? You're supposed to be up there walking or something, aren't you?'

He gestured with his thumb in the direction of the hills, invisible in the thick mist.

'What's the matter?' he added sarcastically. 'Was it too wet for you towny softies?'

I was too cheesed off to rise to the bait, so I told him about the events of the day, and the loss of Lump. Instead of looking concerned, he just burst out laughing.

'What are you laughing at?' I complained angrily.

Ginger and Mave just laughed all the more. I had never seen them happy before. A funny thing to be happy about, I thought.

All Ginger could manage to say was, 'I think you should go to the chip shop.'

Then he and Mave walked off, holding each other up!

I looked at Sparky, who looked back at me, equally confused..

'What do we do now?' I asked.

'Well, what about taking a look at the chip shop?' he replied. 'What have we got to lose?'

It wasn't just curiosity that led me to agree. By now my stomach was ready for food.

The chip shop was at the other end of the village, and, turning the bend in the road, I could see the sign ahead.

Outside was a huddled figure, enjoying what he had bought. It made my mouth water to think of hot chips with lashings of vinegar. My pace speeded up at the thought. As we got nearer, I thought I recognized the eater. It was Lump!

We broke into a run. When we reached him, I grabbed his arm, spinning him round and spraying chips all over the floor.

'What are you doing?' I screamed at him.

He looked startled. 'What's the matter with you?' he protested. 'Look what you've done to my chips!'

I flipped! What with all the trouble he'd caused, and the miserable end to a miserable day, I was ready to carve him into tiny little pieces using the wooden fork he was still clutching. What made matters worse, was that he just stood there, wondering what all the fuss was about.

'Have you seen all those mountain rescue

people rushing about the village?' Lump asked innocently. 'Somebody must have got lost.'

I shot him a look that made him go pale.

'When we got back to the village,' Lump continued, 'everybody spread out and I sort of drifted to the back. I was hungry, so I decided to get some chips before returning to the Centre. Doug's not angry, is he? What's the problem, anyway?'

That was too much!

'What's the problem, what's the problem?' I shrieked. 'There's half the climbers in the north of England out on the hills looking for you, the mountain rescue team have been called out and the police, and probably the army by now, for all we know. And you ask what the problem is?'

Lump backed off nervously, looking shocked.

'Oh dear,' he said, in a pathetic voice.

As I grabbed him by the collar, he cringed.

'Er, don't you think you're going a bit over the top?' Sparky asked from a safe distance.

I grabbed Lump's collar even tighter, and then eased off as I began to calm down a bit.

'I think we all ought to go back to the Centre and sort this out,' Sparky said.

He turned away and began to set off in that direction.

'Well, are you coming or not?' he called over his shoulder.

We followed with different degrees of reluctance, Lump giving me a particularly wide berth.

As we approached the Centre, Doug saw us coming and ran towards us.

'What? . . . Where? . . . How? . . .' was all he

could gasp.

'Never mind that now,' Sparky interrupted. 'Don't you think we ought to get the rescue team back?'

Without answering Doug turned on his heels to go and get everyone recalled and sorted out.

By the time everybody had returned and the whole story had been told, they all agreed it was 'just one of those things' and were simply relieved that no one was hurt.

But not me!

I was still furious.

I was mad with Lump for being so stupid.

I was mad with Doug for getting us into the mess in the first place.

I was mad with Sparky for stopping me thumping Lump.

I was mad with everybody for not being mad.

And I was mad with myself for being mad!

As we walked away from the Centre I could feel myself boiling up inside like a coke bottle which has been shaken up. I blew my top.

'Why have you brought us here, Doug? Is this a prize or a punishment?' I complained. 'Because I've had enough. I'm fed up and want to go home.'

The others all went quiet. Doug grabbed my arm, stopped me, and looked me straight in the eye. 'Everybody else is having a reasonable time, except for the occasional problem,' he said. 'You, as usual, are going right over the top about anything that doesn't go exactly how you like it. Then you start complaining that being a Christian doesn't work. It works for Sparky, doesn't it?'

I didn't say anything but I had to agree.

'It works for me,' Doug went on. 'The trouble is that you want it, like everything else, on your terms. Being a Christian is more than just saying you are one — it has to be worked at like anything else. If you want to be good at football, you have to practise. It's just the same.'

I was flabbergasted. He was right.

He was right, and I didn't like it.

I couldn't think of anything to say, so I ran off towards the camp, feeling like a real wally.

9

GORGEOUS GEORGINA

The next day I got the feeling that everybody was avoiding me so I just lay in my tent feeling sorry for myself.

Suddenly there was a call from outside.

'Go away,' I grumped.

The tent-flap flew open.

'I didn't hear that,' Sam said as she climbed in, followed by Little Mo.

'Hi, big brother,' Mo greeted me cheerfully.

'Get lost,' I replied.

They just kept on talking and ignoring my grumpiness.

'All that business over Lump was really stupid, wasn't it?' Little Mo went on.

I sat up, looked coldly at her, then fell back. 'Why don't they go away?' I thought. But they wouldn't give in.

'We thought you might like to come for a walk,' Sam said.

'No thanks,' I grunted.

'Oh, come on,' Little Mo went on. 'Dad'll be really mad if he thinks you haven't been looking after me, especially when I tell him you wouldn't even take me out for a walk.'

'You rat,' I replied sharply, sitting up. She was using blackmail. I knew there was no way I could get out of it. Grudgingly I gave in.

'All right,' I said, getting up. 'Let's get on with it.'

It was a nice day and as we walked I gradually relaxed, letting my bad feelings go to the back of my mind. There was no one to shout at or push around and it was hard to keep angry.

We were walking along a narrow lane with high walls, which skirted round the edge of Staples farm. We leant on a gate at a gap in the wall and looked across the fields. It was great! Then, about two fields away, I noticed a lorry.

'That's odd. I didn't know Mr Staples had a lorry like that,' I said to Sam. Then we saw some men with big sticks cornering a sheep. It was the sheep thieves!

Before I could work out what to do, one of the men saw us watching them. He pointed in our direction and they quickly left the sheep and ran for the lorry.

I leaped the gate and made off after them, followed by Sam and Mo. Suddenly there was a 'BANG!' and we dived to the ground. I heard the lorry making off, then turned to see Mr Staples standing at the side of the field, a smoking gun in his hands. He didn't look very pleased.

'What on earth are you playing at?' he shouted angrily. 'I nearly caught the blighters. Why did you have to get in the way?'

'Charming,' I replied angrily. 'We didn't know you were there. All we could think about was saving your blinking sheep, and this is all the thanks we get!'

He wasn't in a mood to discuss the point, and Sam, seeing my face and knowing what I was like, interrupted.

'We're ever so sorry, Mr Staples, but honestly we were only trying to help,' she said, and, together with Mo, pushed me towards the gate and back to the road.

I wasn't in the mood to carry on with the walk, so we went back to the camp. It wasn't just that I was angry. I had seen something else that I hadn't told Mr Staples about, and I needed to think.

That moment when I had looked up and seen Mr Staples, I had also seen, further down the road and obscured from him by a hedge, Tom, Ginger and Mave. They had disappeared immediately but I had seen them.

What were they up to?

Were they involved after all?

The next day was an important one on Staples farm. It was the day for sheep-dipping, and we had been invited to go and watch. We were even getting breakfast cooked by Mrs Staples.

In the huge farmhouse kitchen we had as much bacon and eggs as we could handle, sitting round an enormous table. Mr Staples sat at one end behind a newspaper.

'Morning, Mr Staples,' Mo chirped.

'Hmmm,' he grunted in reply from behind the paper. And then to no one in particular, 'I hope everybody's on time.'

Why is it that grown-ups like to communicate in a morning from behind a newspaper? Is it that they can't stand the sight of anybody at that time? Or is it a way of hiding their faces because they look so awful in the morning, before a shave or putting on their make-up? My dad always picks his nose behind his newspaper. Disgusting!

First the sheep were gathered in from the large field they had been put in the day before and put into large pens.

'Where's Frank?' Mr Staples complained. 'He's never around when you want him.'

Before long we saw him coming along the lane, looking very bedraggled. For all his friendliness, there was something about him that I didn't like. But my eyes wandered quickly to somebody else following him down the drive. It was the most beautiful girl I had ever seen, with long blonde hair, and dressed in riding gear.

'Who's that?' I said to nobody in particular.

'Why, bless you, love, it's my niece, Georgina,' Mrs Staples said from behind me. She walked up to the girl to say hello.

After a while, Mrs Staples went in and Georgina wandered over to us.

'Hello,' she said, 'I'm Georgina. Who are you?'

I smiled weakly at her and opened my mouth, but nothing came out.

'He's called Wally,' Mo said, looking hard at me.

'Hello, Wally,' she gushed.

Sam and Mo fell about laughing. I could feel a blush gradually rising up my face, as I turned the colour of a cooked tomato. I couldn't do anything about it.

'No, Georgina,' Sam eventually said. 'That's Mo's joke. He's her brother, Nick.'

'Oh,' replied Georgina blankly.

'Are you here to help with the sheep?' Sam

went on.

'No fear,' she responded quickly. 'Dirty smelly things. I much prefer horses. I've just come to pick up some eggs.'

It was a mouth-before-brain situation, and before I knew it my mouth had put me in a situation I was going to regret.

'I prefer horses, too,' I chipped in.

'Can you ride?' Georgina asked innocently.

'Yes,' I continued, as if it was the only word I knew.

'Liar,' muttered Mo under her breath, but loud enough for me to hear.

I wasn't strictly lying. I *had* ridden a horse — once. When it was the police open day I had been given a lesson on a police horse. Well, actually, it was twenty minutes riding round a field with someone leading.

Georgina perked up at my reply.

'Oh lovely,' she said. 'Would you like to come for a ride with me tomorrow?'

'Great,' I replied. Caught!

Then she tripped off to collect the eggs.

'Oh no,' groaned Mo. Sam just looked hostile.

We watched the sheep being guided down a narrow concrete channel filled with liquid. As soon as Georgina reappeared at the door I hoped I looked like a macho farm-worker.

'See you tomorrow then,' she called. 'I live at Valley Farm. You can't miss it. It's about a mile down the lane from here.'

I waved. Whizzer groaned. Sam looked like thunder!

I was so busy looking at Georgina and desperately trying to think of something to say, that I stepped forward, not noticing the sheep-dip in front of me. I suddenly lost sight of Georgina as I cartwheeled into the dip.

I surfaced among the sheep to see a crowd of laughing faces looking down at me. Did *I* feel embarrassed! They helped me out and I made a run for it.

After a short while Sam appeared round the corner of the barn. I couldn't look at her.

'I've no sympathy,' she said. 'You've made a complete wally of yourself and I should leave you to rot, but Mr Staples says you should be cleaned up as soon as possible, so just stand still.' Wondering what was going to happen next, I stood dripping against the wall. With a glint in her eye as cold as steel, Sam reappeared round the corner holding a hose in her hands!

Before I could take evasive action someone turned it on, and I was getting my second soaking of the day. This one was even wetter than the first, and Sam was none too gentle about it.

The next day dawned bright and clear. After all the things that had gone wrong, I had real hopes that the day would be a good one! After all, I was going out riding with 'gorgeous Georgina'.

At the back of my mind there was the slight niggle that I really didn't know how to ride a horse — but I could ride a bike, and it didn't look much different. Anyway, the old 'Baker magic' should see me through!

I wasn't getting on too well with the rest of the gang. Everybody seemed to be in a funny mood

73

except me! The rest of the lads had gone wandering off downstream from the camp to play near a bridge that was a great spot for paddling. I didn't know where the girls had gone. I think Doug was asleep in his tent.

I combed my hair and put on some clean jeans and set off down the lane towards Georgina's farm, dreaming of riding along with the wind rushing through my hair, Georgina trying to keep up on her smaller pony, just like an advert on TV.

'PAARRP!!'

The noise shook me awake, and I leaped for the wall by the side of the road as a lorry whooshed past. It wasn't until it had gone that I realized it was the lorry I had seen in the field when Mr Staples fired his gun. And by the time I struggled to my feet, I also realized it was the same lorry that had run down Tom.

'If I was Sherlock Holmes, it would be easy,' I muttered as I dusted myself off and carried on walking.

Suddenly the silence was broken by another unexpected noise.

10

ANOTHER FINE MESS!

'Whiiii, wheeeeew!'

It was Sparky, I'd know that wolf-whistle any-where.

I had reached a bridge over the same stream that ran past our campsite. Looking down I could see Sparky, Whizzer, Raj, Chip, and Lump paddling in the stream.

'Who's a pretty boy, then?' Sparky yelled.

'Going somewhere special?' added Whizzer, sarcastically.

I bent down, picked up the biggest boulder I could find, and lobbed it into the stream beside them. It landed with a terrific 'SPLASH!' and they had no time to get out of the way.

'Ugh!' 'Yuk!' 'Oh no,' they yelped in chorus.

I leaned on the bridge, looked down, and smiled at them.

'You look a bit wet,' I said. 'Has it been raining?'

They started to splash water in my direction, and I ducked for cover.

'Peace!' I yelled from behind the bridge wall, and the barrage of water stopped. I carefully and slowly raised my head to look down, holding a boulder in my hand in case of a double cross.

'OK. Peace,' Sparky replied, looking apprehen-sively at the boulder in my hand. I put it down and started to climb down to them. Then I noticed Old Tom walking along the path by the stream towards us all.

'Hello, lads,' he said. 'Doing a bit of fishing, are we?'

'Going for a swim more like,' I laughed, pointing out the others' wet clothes.

Whizzer kicked some water in my direction.

'Watch it,' I warned him, jokingly.

'Did you see that lorry go by?' I asked, changing the subject.

'We saw *a* lorry,' Sparky replied.

'That's just it,' I said excitedly. 'I'm sure it belongs to the sheep thieves. But I still couldn't get the number or see who was in the cab.'

'Have *you* seen that lorry before?' I asked Tom.

There was a strange look on Tom's face.

'Look,' he replied, 'I think you should keep away from what's going on.'

'What do you mean?' I responded.

'Never mind,' he continued mysteriously. 'Just enjoy your holiday, go home, and let somebody else sort it out.'

Then, abruptly, he changed the subject.

'Have you caught any fish?' he asked.

'We weren't really trying,' Sparky replied. 'Anyway, we're not quite in your league.'

'What do you mean?' Tom said quickly. 'I gave that game up a long time ago.' He turned to me. 'When I was younger, much younger,' he went on, 'I was a bit of a poacher, but that was a long time ago.'

'How did you catch the fish?' Sparky asked.

'I tickled them,' was Tom's strange reply.

'You're kidding,' Whizzer said, shaking his head.

'No,' Tom said. 'But it wasn't really tickling. One way to do it is to stand in the water with your legs apart and your hands down under the water until the fish swim between. You have to keep very still. Then, when the fish swim over your hands, you lift them quickly, and fling the fish on to the bank.'

The rest of the lads bent down and tried it in the stream.

'Very strange,' muttered Raj.

'It's a funny way of catching tiddlers,' added Sparky.

'I think I'd rather get my fish from the supermarket,' Whizzer concluded. 'Sort of tickle it out of the frozen food department!'

'Hey, Grandad,' we suddenly heard.

Up on the bridge Ginger and Mave had arrived.

'Gotta be going,' Tom said. And with that, he climbed up to his grandchildren and was away without so much as a wave.

'Some folk are very strange,' I said, shaking my head. Then, without thinking of the consequences, added, 'Gotta be going myself. Got a date.'

'Whe-hey,' they all chorused.

I tried to give them one of my best withering looks.

Walking on, I continued down the lane. It took me round Tom's smallholding — a few fields, a cottage, some outbuildings, and part of the wood. Rounding a bend I almost walked straight into the back of an estate car. The tailgate was open, but nobody was about. A very flashy sports car was parked in front of it.

Then I heard voices coming over the wall from one of Tom's fields. Something stopped me from looking over and I hid behind a bush.

I saw two men appear, hopping over the wall and back into the lane. One man had a kind of tripod that I had seen surveyors carry and he put it in the estate car, slamming the tailgate shut.

The other bloke was a real 'medallion man' type, all flashy clothes and jewellery.

'What do you think?' Medallion Man said.

'Perfect,' the other bloke replied. 'When do we start?'

'I need to do a bit of . . . er . . . negotiating first!' Medallion Man replied.

The other bloke laughed and they got into their separate cars and drove off.

When they had gone I came out from behind the bush. 'What on earth was all that about?' I said to myself, shook my head, and once more set off for my 'date'.

I soon arrived at Georgina's house and I made my way along the drive and round the side of the house to the stables. As I walked along I quickly ran my hands through my hair. Yes, I was still the same handsome hunk I had always been!

By the stables 'gorgeous Georgina' was waiting!

'Sorry I'm a bit late,' I apologized.

'That's all right,' she replied. 'I've really been looking forward to our ride together.'

I blushed. I tried not to, but could feel the colour rising up in my face. It was as if somebody had opened up the top of my head and poured

red dye in.

'I've put you a hard hat out,' she went on. 'I hope it fits.'

I tried it on and wondered why it was necessary. It did nothing for my carefully prepared hairstyle.

'By the way,' she said, 'your sister and her friend are already here. They said you wouldn't mind!'

I groaned! Why couldn't they leave me alone?

'The horses are out in the field already,' Georgina added. 'Shall we go?'

'Lead the way,' I said, trying to sound like John Wayne.

I followed her out, like a lamb to the slaughter.

When we got to the field, Sam and Little Mo were leaning on the gate, waiting.

'Here comes Clint Eastwood,' chirped Little Mo.

I gave her one of my looks. I felt a right wally in that helmet, though.

But when I looked at the horse I was going to ride, I suddenly felt very grateful for that hat. The saddle was a long way off the ground!

Georgina was already on her pony and sat waiting.

The moment of truth had arrived. It was at this point that I began to realize that horse-riding wasn't as easy as it looked on TV. But there was no turning back now.

Having watched my fair share of cowboy films I knew what I had to do, vaguely. I got hold of the reins with my left hand, put my left foot in the stirrup, grabbed the saddle, and hopped up. Now, that horse had seemed to be a very well-behaved, friendly sort. He hadn't moved a muscle so far. Until that moment! Just as I hopped, the brute took a careful, measured step forward, knocking me off balance and landing me with perfect aim in the only patch of mud for yards. I swear it looked round and smirked at me. It was just then that I decided I didn't like horses. There I lay, in my best gear, covered in mud, right in front of Little Mo, Sam and, worst of all, Georgina.

Sam and Mo buried their mouths in their sleeves, but I could see their eyes watering.

'I think you missed,' Sam's muffled voice spoke from behind her sleeve.

'Sorry,' Georgina said very apologetically, 'I should have warned you. Dad's horse can be a bit awkward sometimes, but you assured me you were a very experienced rider, so I didn't bother.'

I struggled to my feet and tried to repair my somewhat battered image.

No way was this horse going to beat me. I grabbed the reins and hopped up very quickly this time, before it had time to think of another devious way to land me in the dirt. Gingerly I sat up straight, then smirked down at Sam and my sister.

'Great,' Georgina said. 'Shall we try once round the field to get used to things?'

'OK,' I replied. 'Lead the way.'

She set off at a gentle trot.

'Right,' I said to myself, 'now to get this thing started.'

In the movies I had seen cowboys get their horses going by a sharp dig in the ribs with the heels. Seemed as good a way as any!

I smiled down at Sam, stuck my tongue out at

Mo, and dug hard with my heels.

The effect was electric! The horse bucked furiously, then galloped away.

I passed Georgina at speed, who looked on in amazement, her wave frozen in mid-air. The horse was snorting and bucking. All I could do was hang on tight to the reins. At that point I lost sight of the others.

We were coming to the end of the field. Now, although you see a lot of horses stopping and starting in films, you very rarely see them turning corners. At this point I couldn't remember ever seeing *anybody* turn a corner on a horse.

It was a split-second decision. I decided to let the horse choose which way to go. He chose to leave the field, which meant jumping the fence! I decided to hang on as tight as I could and firmly shut my eyes. I shall never know how we both managed to clear that fence.

When I opened my eyes again I had lost all sense of direction. All I knew was that I was still on top of this mad beast and trees were rushing past me at an alarming speed.

I desperately tried to think how to stop. How did you put on the brakes? It seemed logical to try pulling on the reins, but how hard? In the movies they pulled very hard. I was getting really fed up with this stupid horse, so it was time for decisive action. I grabbed hard on the reins and pulled!

Well, the horse stopped. Boy, was it fitted with good brakes! Only trouble was, the horse stopped quicker than I did. Suddenly I was sailing gracefully through the air.

Another fine mess I'd got myself in to!

11

NICK DOES IT AGAIN!

Flying is best done in an aeroplane. After leaving the horse behind, I was hoping for a soft landing. I got it!

That horse was a brilliant shot. He catapulted me with great precision, right into an enormous pile of cow-muck. I sat up and looked around to see Georgina approaching. She passed me without a glance and went to gather up the reins of her father's horse. She seemed more worried about him than me! After a short time she came back with it in tow.

'Are you all right?' she asked coldly.

I nodded.

'You were lying,' she continued. 'That'll teach me to trust boys! You could have really hurt yourself — and what's more, you could have seriously damaged the horse!'

I smiled weakly at her, but she just turned and walked away back to her own horse.

Up ran Sam and Mo.

'Are you OK?' Sam asked.

'I think so,' I replied, trying to sound fragile.

Little Mo just stood looking scornful as I removed the helmet and shook my head.

'I think — er — you'd better take this back. I don't think I'm exactly flavour of the month with

Georgina.'

'Liars get found out in the end, don't they?' Mo said, rather unkindly, I thought, as she took the helmet.

'Anyway,' Sam went on, 'with the smell you're giving off, you're nobody's flavour of the month.' Then, turning to Mo, she said, 'Come on, let's go.'

They turned and left. I just sat there.

I staggered to my feet and began to clean myself up using a handkerchief and some big dock leaves. But, although I managed to get most of the gunge off, I couldn't get rid of that persistent, long-remembered, stomach-churning smell.

Grimly I looked around for some recognizable landmark to show me the way home. In the end, I just wandered down the path in the direction the girls had taken, hoping that I would find a way that didn't take me past Valley Farm!

I soon heard the sound of a car and saw a road the other side of the next field. There didn't seem much point in worrying about my gear now, so I climbed over a wall, across the next field and over the next wall, to find myself back on the road to the campsite.

I set off gloomily towards the camp. It wasn't long before I was back at the bend before the bridge where Sparky and the rest were playing. I stopped to think.

My — er — unfortunate disagreement with the horse was bound to get out eventually, but just at that moment I couldn't face the teasing. How was I going to get past the stream without being seen?

I could hear the lads making a lot of noise

as they mucked around, so I crept forward cautiously. I could see the low wall of the bridge. Now, if I crouched down and crawled along on my hands and knees, they just might not see me. First I looked through the trees to see where they were. I could see some figures happily messing about throwing stones in the water. Now was my chance!

Crawling along, I was just thinking to myself that I would make a great recruit for a spy film, 003½ perhaps, when . . .

'Hey, Nick, why are you crawling along on your hands and knees? Have you lost something?' It was a voice I instantly recognized. Lump!

My heart sank!

I turned my head, and there he was, sitting up against a tree, stuffing himself with crisps. I put my finger to my lips to tell him to be quiet, but, as usual, he misunderstood — the wally!

'You want one?' Lump said. He struggled to his feet and came over, holding out the packet.

Suddenly he stopped. With a noise that could have been heard the other side of Glasgow he cried, 'PHEW!' and gripped his nose as if it were about to fall off.

'What a pong!' he spluttered through his hand.

Before I had time to move, the others joined us.

'Hey, Nick,' Sparky said, surprised, 'what are you doing?'

'Oh er . . .' I replied lamely. 'I'm er . . . I er . . . dropped something.'

Quick as a flash, Sparky and the others were by my side, keen to help.

'What have you lost, man?' Whizzer asked.

Then suddenly, 'PHEW!' Chip said, stepping back, as did the others, holding their noses.

'What have you done?' Sparky said, then they all burst out laughing.

'All right, all right,' I said. 'Look, I slipped in some muck, OK?'

I wasn't going to tell them exactly what happened. They'd find that out soon enough from Sam and Little Mo, my big-mouth sister.

'What happened to the horse ride?' Whizzer asked innocently.

'Look,' I went on, ignoring the awkward question, 'I've got to get myself cleaned up. I haven't got time to stand here talking to you lot!'

'But what about whatever it was that you lost?' Sparky asked, with a curious look on his face.

I groaned inside. Like all lies, you have to keep on lying to make the story work, and gradually get into deeper and deeper water.

'Yes,' I replied, trying to look worried and desperately trying to think quickly. 'It was my watch. I must have lost it when I came past before and threw that rock at you.'

It was a bit weak, but the best I could do in an emergency. With great energy, like true friends, they immediately began searching all around. I thought I had escaped.

I was just about to say that I must have lost it somewhere else when Sparky sat bolt upright.

'Just a minute,' he suddenly said. 'I went with you to town a few days before we came on holiday to take your watch to be repaired. You never brought it with you!'

Quick as a flash, before anybody had time to

add two and two together and make even more than four, I replied, 'Oh, so did I, how silly of me. Still, that's all solved, so I can go off and clean up now.'

I didn't dare to look at Sparky's face as I turned and made off in the direction of the camp, but I could easily imagine his expression. I could feel his eyes piercing the back of my head as he tried to work out why I had lied, and what it was all about.

My ears burned so much you could have used them to light a fire. As I walked I began to grumble to myself about everything and anything, talking myself in to a mood. I thought about all sorts of horrible things that ought to happen to various people, friends and enemies alike. I also told the trees about how horrible the holiday was and what a vile place Tidesbourne was. What made me feel worse was the fact that everybody else was having a great time. It just wasn't fair!

That old Baker temper was surfacing again!

My mum always said I took after my dad in that. My dad always reckoned I took after my mum. I knew it came from plain old selfish me, but at the moment I didn't want to think about that.

In a grim mood, sunk in gloom, I wandered back till I reached Staples farm.

But my mood soon left me when I saw there was a car outside the farmhouse — a police car. What was up? I ran over, curiosity making me forget everything else.

By the car stood Mr Staples, very angry, with arms waving. Frank and Bill stood alongside and a very patient policeman, his notebook open, was taking notes and nodding his head. He did remind me of my dad, who was a policeman as well.

Nobody noticed me, until I got near. The smell got to them before I did. I could see their noses twitching as they turned to stare at me. Bill came over to me while the others carried on talking.

'Phew, Nick,' he complained, holding his nose. This was getting monotonous. 'You don't half pong,' he continued. 'What have you been doing?'

I had neither the time, nor did I want to tell him what had really happened.

'Never mind,' I said sharply. 'What's going on here?'

'Some sheep gone again,' he replied.

I turned to the others and listened.

'I'm really fed up with all this,' Mr Staples said angrily. 'When are you going to do something about it, that's what I want to know?'

'Look, Mr Staples,' the constable replied, 'I'll make a report and we'll keep a careful look-out. Sooner or later we're bound to catch them.'

'Later is what I'm worried about,' Mr Staples snapped back. 'I'll have no sheep left by then!'

The policeman ignored Mr Staples' anger and carried on writing.

'Now, did anyone see anything suspicious?' he asked generally.

'Well, I saw Old Tom hanging about,' Frank said.

I really didn't like that guy, he was too sly, and I wasn't going to let him get Tom into trouble.

'Just a minute,' I said, stepping forward and

butting in.

Everyone took a step back as I came towards them.

'I saw Old Tom earlier, by the stream, nowhere near here,' I added.

Frank looked hard at me, then asked, 'Which direction was he coming from?'

I knew what he was getting at and didn't want to answer. He was a bit too keen to get Tom into trouble for my liking. The stream passes through Staples farm before it flows by the bridge where the gang were playing, then it goes by Tom's smallholding, then round Valley farm.

Eventually, after a long silence, I admitted, 'Downstream,' trying to make it sound unimportant.

'That proves it,' jumped in Mr Staples. 'I knew that old rogue was involved.'

He turned to the constable. 'What are you going to do about it? Go and arrest the man.'

'All it proves,' replied the policeman patiently, 'is that Tom was near the farm around the time that the sheep went missing. If I arrested everybody who was near here at the time, my little lock-up would be full ten times over. You leave it to me, Mr Staples. I'll have a word with Tom in the next few days. In the meantime, don't worry, we're bound to catch them soon.'

'Bah!' grunted Mr Staples, and stormed into the house. The policeman got into his car and drove off.

'Cor, you really do niff,' Bill said at my side. 'Why don't you go and have a bath or something?'

'Later,' I replied sharply, gave a hard look at

Frank, and turned on my heels. I was determined to find Old Tom and tell him about the policeman.

I ran all the way back to Tom's cottage, not even stopping to talk to the gang who were still at the bridge. The cottage was off the main road, down a long, dark, overgrown lane, all on its own.

I knocked on the door.

No answer.

I knocked again.

Still no answer, but I heard a scuffle from inside.

Something was wrong. What had I walked into?

Suddenly the door opened — just a crack!

12

THE SLIPPERY SNAKE

A voice spoke sharply from behind the door.

'What do you want?' it grunted.

It was Ginger.

'Can I talk to your grandad?' I asked.

'Why?' he replied. 'We don't like nosy parkers.'

'I've got something important to tell him,' I went on.

There was silence. After a while the door opened and Tom put his head round.

'Hello, Nick,' he said. 'What do you want?'

'I came to warn you that some more sheep have been taken from Staples farm. The police were called, and everybody's blaming you.'

'Tell me something new,' Tom laughed. 'But thanks for coming round to tell me.'

There was a long silence as we stood looking at each other.

Then Tom opened the door some more.

'Come on in,' he said.

I was about to step in when I suddenly thought and stopped.

'I pong a bit,' I said. Then, before they got the wrong idea, added, 'I fell in a pile of muck.'

'That won't bother us,' Tom said kindly. 'A bit of muck won't make any difference.'

What I saw when I got inside took my breath

away.

It looked as if a bomb had gone off. There were books, pots, and furniture thrown about all over the place. Ginger and Mave were trying to put things straight.

'What on earth happened here?' I asked, looking around.

'Let's just say we had some visitors who wanted to tell me something!' Tom said mysteriously. Then he put a hand on each of my shoulders and looked me in the eye.

'Now, Nick, I want you to listen very carefully,' he went on. 'I don't want you to ask any more questions about what has happened.'

'But why?' I interrupted.

'Never mind. No more questions, and I don't want you to tell anybody — *anybody* — about what you have seen. Is that clear?' he added.

'OK,' I said doubtfully. I didn't think it was right, but, at that moment I couldn't think of anything else to say. He was a friend, and if that was what he wanted . . .

I set to work helping them to tidy up, trying to put the mystery together in my mind. There were lots of interesting things in the cottage, and every so often Tom would stop to tell me about a particular photograph I had found, or the history of a piece of furniture.

I was desperate to ask questions, but Tom just kept changing the subject. When I left I was no wiser. I was even more puzzled about what was going on. What was Old Tom trying to hide?

One of the highlights of our holiday had been

planned for the next day, and I'd been looking forward to it ever since Doug said he would take us. About twenty miles from the village was the biggest theme park in the country, called 'Beacon Manor', and we were going there for the day. It was one day none of the gang was going to miss. I woke up that morning feeling really excited.

But even as we stood around waiting for Doug to bring the van along, I had a feeling it wasn't going to be my day. Instead of being her usual chatty self, Sam turned her back on me. Over the years we had often fallen out, but we had always made it up before. This time I had really blown it! Nobody seemed that keen on me, but the way Sam was treating me was the worst. She was madder than I had ever seen her.

The journey to the park was as uneventful as any ride could be in that awful boneshaker of a van, but we made it — just! Even though we had set off early, there was still an enormous queue to get in, and then it took ages to find a place in the enormous car park. Through the trees we could see the bright colours of the rides, and the excitement began to fizz up in my stomach. This would be something to boast about next term at school!

We got out of the van and stretched our legs.

'Wow, man. Fantastic,' Whizzer said as he switched off his Walkman. 'What a place, what a place!'

Raj, who rarely said anything, just looked around with his mouth open.

Everybody was looking round, pointing things out to each other. Back home we had talked about how many times we would go on the famous loop-the-loop roller-coaster we had seen on TV, called the 'Slippery Snake'. Seeing it through the trees and hearing the screams and rattling of the cars, some doubts began to creep into our minds. Now we would see who was just talk!

Me — I was ready for anything. It would be a good time to show everybody how tough I was and win back a bit of respect!

I turned to Sam, putting on my best 'macho' manner.

'Come on, Sam, let me take you on the "Pirate Ship". I'll look after you,' I said.

If looks could kill, I would have died on the spot.

'Why don't you go and ride the horses on the merry-go-round, or are you afraid you might fall off?' she replied. Then she turned to Mo. 'Come on, Mo, let's go on the "Pirate Ship", I don't like creeps.'

The rest of the gang fell about laughing.

My heart turned to stone. My jaw dropped so far open it must have nearly reached the ground!

Still laughing, Raj and Whizzer headed off for their first go on the 'Slippery Snake'. Lump waddled off in the direction of a hot dog stall, and Chip made for the electronic games.

I just stood there.

'What about a go on the log flume?' Sparky asked me.

I exploded. 'I can do without your goody-goody sympathy,' I snarled at him. 'Push off and leave me alone.'

Without waiting for a response I turned on my heels and stormed off. Unfortunately, the way I had chosen to go was past the 'Pirate Ship', which was swinging high into the air with its load of screaming passengers. I could clearly see — and hear — Sam and Mo screaming with pleasure.

'I'm not interested in girlfriends, but she shouldn't treat me like that,' I said to myself. I must have said it rather loudly because I got some strange looks from people walking past. That made me feel embarrassed as well as angry. I strode off quickly, seeing a lake ahead with some boats. Fortunately there was no queue, so I paid, stepped into one and rowed furiously out into the lake.

There I could drift into my dreamworld where *I* was in charge, everybody agreed with me, and did exactly as I said.

Reaching the middle of the lake, I pulled in the oars and lay back in the boat, staring up at the sky. Around me all was peaceful, except for the distant squeals coming from the rides, and all I could see was the white clouds drifting across. Boy, was I fed up!

Suddenly, the boat lurched as something hit the side, and there, looking down at me, was Doug.

'What do you want?' I growled. 'I don't want to hear any sermons.'

'Are you all right?' he asked, ignoring my nastiness. 'I was — er — just rowing past and — er — thought I might stop for a chat.'

I glared up at him with a 'Who are you kidding?' look, but I was quite happy to see him really.

I was famous for my 'I want to be alone' trick. 'King of the sulks', my mum said, but I never quite knew what to do with myself after I had stamped off!

'You are a bit of a wally, aren't you?' Doug said.

I just looked at him. What could I say? He was right!

He and Sparky were the best friends I had, and they stuck with me whatever I was like. I suppose that's what being a real friend is. If I were Doug, I would have walked away from me and left me to rot — if you see what I mean! But Doug never did.

'Any mess you get in is usually your own doing, you know,' he went on. 'Then you expect your friends to forgive and forget — when you don't even do it yourself.'

He didn't have to remind me about that again, I knew all too well. I knew that I had to do something about it, too. I just didn't want to!

But I still didn't answer.

'A suggestion,' he continued. 'To begin with, how about swallowing your pride and saying sorry to Sam for the way you treated her? You might then try and think about letting your friends be the kind of pals *they* want to be, instead of how *you* want them to be.'

He didn't say anything else, but rowed off, leaving me to think about what he'd said. The battle was on — would I be able to swallow my pride and apologize?

I wasn't very good at it, but not many people are. It's dead easy when you're at fault to think of all the things wrong with everybody else and forget your own mistakes.

I sat up, flicking the water with my fingers,

remembering my pals, and all the things we had done together. I remembered a lot of the scrapes I had got into and all the times Sparky and the rest had been on hand to rescue me. For some daft reason I remembered the time when we were little and I got my head stuck in the park railings. Sparky and Sam between them kept me calm, just, while the fire engines came. I laughed to myself.

And then I thought back to last year. When Sparky said he was a Christian, I thought that would be the finish between us. But it wasn't. He became an even better friend, in spite of me!

What should I do? I wasn't going to enjoy it, but I had to make things up with Sam for a start.

I pulled myself together and rowed slowly back to the boathouse area, trying to think of the best way to apologize. Whatever I thought of, it sounded really stupid. I guess any apology sounds stupid to the one doing the apologizing.

First, I had to find her.

There she was, queuing for the 'Parachute Jump' with Mo. I didn't know whether to wait, or get on with it. But, figuring I might chicken out if I waited, I decided now was the time.

Marching up to them in the queue I could see that they hadn't noticed me. Sam didn't seem very happy, sort of bored and cross!

I tapped Sam on the shoulder, and she turned and looked at me blankly.

Words failed me. My mouth opened and shut but nothing came out.

'Yes?' she said coldly. 'What do you want?'

'Er — I — er,' I stuttered. 'Can we talk?'

'Go ahead,' she responded. 'I'm all ears.'

'Not here,' I said defensively.

'If you think I'm going to lose my place in the queue for you,' she went on, 'you've got another think coming.'

A large man behind them suddenly grabbed my shoulder.

''Ere,' he said, 'we'll 'ave no queue jumpin'. You get to the back.'

He was too big to argue with. I had to get on with it.

This was awful!

13

NICK & CO. ON THE TRAIL

I turned to Sam.

'Look,' I blurted out. 'I want to say, I'm sorry for the way I treated you.'

Sam looked at me.

'I treated you badly, sorry,' I went on.

'Are you going to move?' the man behind me said. 'Or will I have to move you?'

I grabbed Sam's hand and pulled her out of the queue.

'I think I'll go and find Doug,' Mo said, smiling. What a great sister!

Sam and I stood looking at each other. Eventually she spoke.

'You ever do that again, and I'll kill you,' she said.

'What about a go on the "Slippery Snake"?' I asked. She nodded. We sat off in that direction.

It wasn't until I heard loud whistles and shouts from above that I realized I was still holding Sam's hand. It was Sparky, Whizzer and Raj up in the cable car above us, pointing and making a lot of noise.

I quickly drew away my hand and shoved it in my pocket. Sam looked at me and burst out laughing.

'You are daft,' she said. 'Come on, let's get in

the queue.'

We spent the rest of the day very happily on the white-knuckle rides. We all had a great time, and even got Doug to go on them. I wasn't sure if it was the sort of thing vicars ought to do, but he said it was quite all right.

In the middle of the afternoon we had a big meal in a café, where Lump in particular packed away a huge lunch. I didn't do too badly, either!

Then after lunch it was back on the rides — the gentler ones to start off with. I didn't fancy seeing my lunch return. At the end of the day we had to have one last go on the 'Slippery Snake'. We even got Lump to go on it. He had been avoiding it all day. It was a great machine, with twists and turns, and a loop-the-loop that sent your stomach up to your throat and down to your boots in turn.

We had thought that was the perfect end to the day. Then Doug, who was pleased to see us all happy, bought us all waffles, piled high with everything sweet and sickly you could think of. Lump had looked a bit green when he came off the 'Snake', but he could never resist food . . . which would have been fine, except Sparky suggested one quick last go on the 'Pirate Ship'.

We all thought it was a great idea and dragged Lump along as well. He was *very* reluctant, but before he had time to argue we were all on, and the swaying had begun. Higher and higher we climbed, and as the screams got louder, Lump's face got greener. That lovely feeling at the top of the swing when you leave your stomach behind must have been agony. I took a look at him. I didn't think he would get off without 'unloading the dumptruck', so to speak.

He might have been reluctant to get on, but he was *very* quick to get off, rushing for some nearby bushes. When he had recovered we set off home in the van, although nobody wanted to sit next to our green-faced friend. We actually got nearly home before Lump yelled for us to stop, and dashed into some trees to be sick. I recognized the place — it was near where we stopped on the way to Tidesbourne with the puncture.

We all got out and were standing around waiting, when Sparky caught my arm and pointed down the road. In the distance we could see that lorry again — I was sure it was the same one! We hadn't told Doug about all the things we had seen, and he couldn't understand when we tried to get everybody back in the van and go in pursuit.

By the time Lump had sorted himself out and we had set off, there was no sign of the lorry. It must have disappeared into thin air.

Suddenly there was a 'PAARRP', and Doug gripped the wheel tightly in surprise.

We dived to the back window and looked out. Trying to get past us was a great, flashy, open car with two people in it. It wasn't just the driver that I recognized, but the passenger as well. It was Grabber! Medallion Man was driving, in the car that I had seen on the way to Georgina's!

We waved our fists at them and the driver blew on the horn and squeezed up against the van with his car. The road was very narrow, but that didn't stop him, and Doug had to take avoiding action. We lurched along with two wheels on the verge and Doug slewed the van to a halt.

Poor Lump had to leap out to be sick again with all the jolting about we had taken.

The car didn't stop, but drove on at speed, its horn blaring.

'What a stupid driver!' Doug said.

Sparky and I just looked at each other!

It was a lovely day for our last Sunday in Tidesbourne. We were taking part in the morning service at the church, by doing some drama. Doug's fancy clothes, which vicars wear for such occasions, looked whiter than white. You could have used him for a washing powder advert.

We were going to act out two scenes from the Bible about the life of one of Jesus' close friends, called Peter. And I was playing the part of Peter.

Before we started rehearsing Doug said that he couldn't think of anybody better to play the part. I *think* it was because I am good at acting, but Sparky's laugh made me wonder! *And* Doug's answering smile.

The first scene was the one where Jesus was in the garden of Gethsemane and the men came to arrest him. Sparky was playing Jesus and Whizzer played the soldier who got his ear cut off when Peter tried to stop them. That was good — except that I nearly *did* take Whizzer's ear off with the wooden sword. It was a good job I didn't manage it because, good as Sparky was, I don't think he'd have been able to put it back on for real, like Jesus did!

The second scene was when Peter denied he knew Jesus three times, after Jesus had been arrested — and then the cock crowed, just as

Jesus had told Peter it would. That went well, except for Raj getting too carried away. He was doing the crowing of the cockerel from the back of the church, and nearly gave the old ladies heart attacks, he was so loud and unexpected!

I really liked Peter. When he first knew Jesus he was always opening his mouth and putting his foot in it. But Jesus stuck with him, kept forgiving him and helping him, and eventually Peter became the leader of all the Christians at the time.

Doug talked for a bit at the end of the drama, about how Peter started off being a bit of a loud-mouthed aggressive sort of a guy, and then learned through Jesus about how that wasn't the best way of going about things. I felt as if Doug was looking straight at me all the time he was saying this. But I didn't care! I reckoned that if Peter could survive all that and finish up the way he did, so could I. And I knew that Jesus wouldn't give up on me.

After the service we stood outside and shook people's hands, which was all right, except for the sweaty ones! Some of the old people looked at me a bit strangely and said things like, 'Very nice!' and 'How interesting!'

I wandered off on my own to go back to the camp. As I walked down the lane, I thought about what Doug had been saying, and tried to sort out in my mind all the things that had happened since arriving in Tidesbourne.

It's dead easy to lose your cool and crash about like Peter did. But in the end, Peter had to stop behaving like that. It was a bit like me really. I guess in the end I had to do what Doug was always going on about — to calm down and not be ashamed to ask for God's help. Talking to God wasn't that hard really. It was only embarrassing if you didn't really believe it worked. So, quietly, on my own, I asked God to forgive me for being so stupid — and to help me change.

Before I knew it I had arrived at the bridge where the gang liked to mess around, but there was no fun going on there this time. As I got nearer I could hear voices. Now, it's not that I'm nosy but, just like most people would, I found myself walking very quietly, trying to pick up some of the conversation.

What's more, I noticed, further on, that sports car that had nearly made us have an accident in the van. Now I was really curious!

Quietly, I raised my head over the parapet of the bridge and looked down. Below me, and leaning against the stonework of the bridge, was Ginger. Facing him, and stopping him from getting away, was that grotty pig, Grabber and the man from the car — Medallion Man.

They were both having a real go at Ginger. I couldn't pick up exactly what they were going on about but I saw enough to know that Ginger was in trouble.

'Just tell that grandfather of yours to do as he's told and keep his mouth shut, or it won't just be your dad that gets dealt with,' I heard Medallion Man say.

There was a lot of prodding and pushing going on. I had to do something to help, but what? I didn't want to get caught myself. Looking round,

I saw a large stone lying by the road, and remembering the effect it had on my pals the other day, I picked it up, aimed carefully and threw it down alongside Grabber.

It had the desired effect.

'Run for it,' I yelled at Ginger, and he didn't need telling twice. He was off down the path like a scalded rabbit. Medallion Man was too worried about his gear to think about chasing, but Grabber clambered up the bank after me.

I made off down the lane as fast as I could, hoping to get far enough ahead not to be caught. Grabber chased me for a bit, but eventually gave up. I stopped running and turned round. We looked at each other from some distance apart on the road.

He pointed his finger at me. 'You stay out of this,' he threatened. 'Or you'll regret it.'

I put my hand to my nose and waved a very rude goodbye before running off in the direction of Staples farm.

At the farm I was in for another surprise. In the yard was the estate car that I had seen with the surveying gear in it. The man who had been nosing about Tom's fields was talking to Mr Staples. I waited for the man to leave then went over to Mr Staples.

'What do you want?' he asked suspiciously.

'I was wondering what that man was doing,' I replied.

He sighed heavily. 'Don't you ever mind your own business?' he grumbled.

There wasn't a lot I could say to that, so I just stood there twiddling a bit of straw, figuring he would either tell me eventually or tell me to push off.

'I called him in to work out how to pull up my part of the wood and what to do with the land. He's an estate agent,' he said eventually.

Then, before I could start arguing with him about the wood, he carried on. 'While he was here he also offered to buy the whole farm,' he continued. 'A very generous offer.'

'But you can't sell,' I replied.

'Why not?' asked Mr Staples. 'If I wait much longer I'll be out of business anyway!'

I wanted to talk to him, to tell him about the things I had found out, but he just walked away sadly. I don't think he would have believed me anyway. But I had to do something.

In the evening we all went for a walk into the village. We stopped and sat down by the pond. Doug was going off to see his mum and dad, and had threatened us with various tortures like extra washing-up, if we got into any bother. As usual Lump got into bother chasing food. He had some sandwiches in his pocket and Whizzer did the unforgivable. He sneaked the sandwiches out of Lump's pocket and launched them out into the middle of the village pond on a piece of wood. You should have seen Lump's face when he saw his precious food sailing into the distance. He went berserk! He ran up and down the edge of the pond like a wild man, screaming abuse at Whizzer.

'You pig, Whizzer, you swine,' he shouted.

He was uncontrollable, getting redder and redder in the face. There was no way he would give up the idea of getting his snack back, but he had some competitors who also had their eyes on the goodies. The ducks on the pond had taken note of the free lunch sailing out into the middle of their own particular dining area and, never ones to refuse a hand-out, were making a beeline for Lump's sandwiches.

Lump now diverted his anger away from Whizzer and towards the ducks.

'Go away, you stupid ducks,' he screamed. 'They are *my* sandwiches.'

At the same time he jumped up and down in anger. I kept wondering what the odds were on him starting an earthquake!

The ducks took no notice, so Lump took drastic action. Without thinking of the consequences he leapt out into the pond, fully clothed!

He beat the ducks to the sandwiches by a short head. They obviously thought he was some sort of large duck trespassing on their territory and his return from the centre of the pond was even quicker than the outward journey, the ducks in hot pursuit!

Lump had the sandwiches, very wet trousers, and filthy shoes!

When I had stopped laughing, I felt really sorry for him, and, much to the amazement of the rest of the gang, lent him my sweater because he was looking a bit cold.

We had decided that while Doug wasn't about we would have a look around to see if we could find out some more about what was going on. Mr and Mrs Staples were out as well so it seemed an ideal time. Sparky wasn't that keen, but I convinced him that we wouldn't do anything illegal.

106

Also, Sam threatened to throw her brother in the pond if he didn't shut up!

We split up into small groups to cover the area around Staples farm, where most of the sheep had been stolen from.

Chip, as the technical expert, had thought up a system of communication using different numbers and types of yells. It all sounded good when he explained it, but I had my doubts. Still, we could only try!

'OK, gang, split up and let's see what we can find,' I told them. Then added, 'And if all else fails, just yell anything as loud as you can!'

I hoped that this general nosing around would lead to something.

As usual, we got more than we bargained for!

14

EVIDENCE

We split up in pairs and went off in different directions. Before long, I was sure, Nick and Co. would be hot on the trail. Someone was bound to come up with a good clue, or see something suspicious.

I set off with Sparky. We were heading towards the back of the wood where I first met Old Tom. It was a lovely evening and there were birds singing in the trees.

'Great, isn't it?' I said to Sparky.

'Yes, smashing,' he replied. 'But you've changed your tune,' he added. I was about to start telling him about why I felt different when something happened.

The trouble with the countryside is that the animals, in this case cows, have a nasty habit of leaving what my little sister Mo calls 'country pancakes' all over the place. Once again I found myself magnetically drawn to things that didn't smell nice! Before I knew what was happening I slipped in some muck and landed flat on my back, looking up into Sparky's laughing face.

'I'd better not say anything, had I?' he said, smirking down at me.

'You'd better not!' I replied.

I got back on my feet and cleaned up the

damage. I was getting good at this!

Suddenly I heard a shout and Sam came rushing towards me, closely followed by Mo. She was pointing towards a hilltop at the other end of the farm, in the direction that Lump and Chip had gone.

We all hurtled off in that direction, clearing gates and stiles like Olympic athletes, and diving through hedges with no thought for the scratches. On the way we picked up Raj and Whizzer who had also heard the shout.

I reached the hilltop first, completely breathless, to be met by Lump and Chip, looking confused and upset. Yes, they'd done it again!

Lump had been startled by a sheep and barged into Chip, who had bounced off into a patch of nettles. The effect of a sudden stinging sensation in the rear caused Chip to scream. He wasn't amused when we asked him why he hadn't used the correct coded shout for a nettle sting in the backside!

We all spread out again and carried on searching. Sparky and I walked back across the farm, this time a bit more slowly.

We started to look around in the wood. Then Sparky grabbed my arm.

'Not Lump again,' I groaned.

'No,' Sparky replied. 'Didn't you hear it?'

I listened. He was right. From the area where Whizzer and Raj had gone there was a clear shout. Two steady shouts, which meant, 'Come quick, we've found something.' Once again we rushed towards the shout.

Whizzer was waiting for us by a wall.

'Over here,' he yelled.

We followed him round the back of the wall to where Raj was standing in a field of sheep looking at something.

'I heard the noise of a big truck,' Raj said. 'But it had gone before we got here.'

'Look,' Whizzer went on, 'there's some wheel tracks.' He pointed to some marks in the mud at the gate to the field. But that wasn't much help. As Sparky pointed out, it could have been one of the farm vehicles.

We also found some scraps of sheep's wool and signs of some sort of struggle, but nothing that could really prove anything There was nothing else to see, apart from a scrap of blue cloth that Sam noticed caught on some barbed wire.

'I think we'd better go and tell Bill,' Sparky said. I couldn't argue with that. Bill was looking after things while Mr and Mrs Staples were out.

We all trooped back to the farmhouse and told Bill the story. When they returned, Mr Staples wasn't pleased, which I thought was a bit unfair because we had *nearly* caught whoever was taking the sheep. He just went on about us taking the law into our own hands, and what would our parents say if we got into bother, and stuff like that. Although the police had promised to keep a close watch over the farm, they weren't interested in our 'evidence'.

I'll never understand grown-ups!

Before bedtime Sparky, Sam, Mo, Whizzer, Raj and I met up in the village for a quick knock at cricket. Raj and Whizzer in particular were dead keen. Whizzer fancied himself as the next demon West Indian fast bowler, and Raj was an ace batsman.

Using a tree for wickets we played with everybody batting and bowling in turn, and no sides. It was my turn to bowl:

'And now, from the Trent Bridge end, coming in to bowl is the latest successor to Ian Botham, the new find for England, Nick Baker.'

'Get on with it,' Sparky complained from the other end, leaning on his bat, waiting for me to come out of fantasy-land.

I ran in to bowl and he played the ball away for Whizzer to chase and throw back. Eventually I got him out, yelling at a non-existent umpire!

Whizzer was an incredibly fast bowler, and he got us all out, one after the other. It may only have been a tennis ball, but he could make it come at you so fast you could hardly see it.

We had been playing for about twenty minutes when that flashy sports car whistled past us and stopped at the village chip shop. We all watched as Grabber and Medallion Man bought some chips.

'Come on,' complained Raj. 'Never mind them, let's get on with the game.'

It was my turn to bat again and I took up my position at the crease, not noticing that Grabber had wandered over. It was Sam's turn to bowl and she was very good, getting me out the next ball, and I didn't play soft because she was a girl!

'What a Noddy!' Grabber called out from the side. 'Getting out to a girl. Is that the best you can do?' He didn't stop there. Leaning on a wall he continued to take the mickey out of me.

'I thought you were a bit soft when you fell over in the race,' he went on. 'Now I'm sure of it. Come on, give me the ball and I'll show you how to play.'

'Right, Dad,' he called to the man by the car. 'Watch this!'

So that was who Medallion Man was!

Grabber snatched the ball from Sam and went over to the bowler's mark. From the area of the chip shop we heard Grabber's dad cheering, and Grabber waved back in salute. They were obviously trying to wind us up.

'Come on,' he demanded. 'Somebody bat. It won't be for long!'

I handed the bat over to Sparky who was next man in. Grabber came rushing in and sent the ball down very fast, hit Sparky hard on the leg, and really hurt him. To add insult to injury he also claimed that Sparky was out leg before wicket. I was just starting to argue when Raj stopped me, winked, and said loudly, 'I'm next.'

Grabber leered nastily at him and said, 'Great, I always like to sort you "foreigners" out.'

What a stupid thing to say! For a start, Raj wasn't a foreigner, he was born in the same hospital as me! And anyway, it really gets on my nerves how some people think that the colour of a person's skin makes him different from anybody else.

Grabber came in again to bowl and Raj stood waiting with the bat. The ball flew down the pitch and *Wham!*, Raj walloped it into the distance.

'A four, I think,' Raj said politely as Mo went off

112

to retrieve the ball. The next three balls went just as far and Grabber was getting angry! He sent down the next ball at head height and not even Raj could reach it. It just missed his face and he fell as he dodged it.

I was in a mood to go over and get Grabber, but Whizzer stopped me.

'Leave this one to me,' he said.

We helped Raj out of the way and sat him down to recover.

'Why don't you have a bat?' Whizzer suggested to Grabber.

'OK,' Grabber replied sarcastically. 'Do you think you can get me out, then?'

'I'll have a go,' Whizzer said. 'If you don't mind a "foreigner" bowling at you, that is.'

Grabber just sneered at him.

Boy, if I had been Whizzer I would have gone for his throat!

Grabber got himself ready to bat and Whizzer ran up to bowl with his steady run, then whirled his arm over fast and, before Grabber knew it, the ball had hit the tree.

'Howzat!' we all yelled.

'I wasn't ready,' Grabber lied.

'Boy, what a cheat,' I thought.

Whizzer looked at him, took the ball, and set off to bowl again.

The next ball bounced up wickedly and hit Grabber right in his stomach. He yelped in pain and doubled up.

'This pitch isn't safe to play on,' he whined.

I was really ready to take the mickey out of him now, but my attention was suddenly taken by his blue shirt. It had a huge rip in it. What's more, it was exactly the same colour material as that piece on the barbed wire at the farm!

Grabber noticed my stare. He looked guiltily at me, then without saying another word went over to his dad and they drove off.

'Why did he have to go so soon? I was just beginning to enjoy myself,' Whizzer joked.

I told them about the tear in Grabber's shirt and reminded them of the piece of cloth on the barbed wire.

'I think things are beginning to fall into place nicely,' I said.

The others just raised their eyebrows and groaned. 'Elementary, my dear Watson,' I said, puffing on an imaginary pipe.

15

OLD TOM VANISHES

The next morning Mr Staples came over to our campsite to see us.

'Oh no!' I groaned under my breath, expecting another ticking off for something or other.

He must have read my mind.

'Don't worry!' he called. 'You haven't done anything wrong. I just wanted a word.'

This was adult-speak for a lot of words!

'I wanted to finish off what I was saying yesterday,' he went on. 'I didn't want you to think I wasn't grateful for what you tried to do. But I was worried for you. You must remember that while you are staying here you are my responsibility. What would your father have said if you had got hurt?'

I dreaded to think! Dad always seemed to 'flip his lid' at the way I attracted trouble like a magnet. To my way of thinking, there was nothing I could do about it, but my dad and now Mr Staples obviously didn't agree with me.

'I still don't think Old Tom had anything to do with it,' I said, changing the subject.

Mr Staples sighed and raised his eyebrows.

'Maybe you're right, Nick,' he replied. 'But you must admit, he always seems to be around when something happens.'

That was true, but I was sure that there was a reason for that, something I hadn't figured out yet.

I looked across at Doug, who didn't know much about what had been happening. He had a funny look on his face.

When Mr Staples left, Doug turned on me. 'Right,' he demanded. 'What's been going on, then?'

'Sparky will tell you,' I replied quickly. 'Got to go and . . . er . . . post a card.'

Before I could be stopped I hurried off, avoiding Sparky's eyes. I'd landed him in it, as usual! I was really keen to see Tom and find out a bit more about what was going on, so I decided to go to his house. By the time I reached it, I had a list of questions in my head to ask him. But I never got the chance!

I should have realized that something was wrong the moment I reached the gate. The front door was open, and I knew that wasn't right.

'Hello,' I called round the door. 'Is anybody ho-ome?'

There was no response and I began to get nervous but, being Nick Baker, I had to go on. I pushed the door open and made my way inside. There was no one about. I looked into every room but there was no sign of life. But there were signs of some kind of a fight. The lounge looked like my bedroom after a pillow-fight with my sister Mo.

Straight away I was convinced they were in trouble and I had to do something. I turned on my heels and ran to the village to find help.

I went to find the village bobby, who was sitting in a deckchair admiring his garden. He seemed a nice guy, but very slow, the original P.C. Plod. I told him about what I had seen, but he obviously didn't want to move.

'Tom does that sometimes,' he said from the comfort of his chair. 'He'll be back, don't you worry. He's probably heard about some hurt animal or something, and rushed off to help. That's what the mess will be about and why the door was open. I've been up there a few times myself and found it like that, and he's always returned.'

I was only half convinced, but there was no way that this guy was going to move. I don't think he would have moved if half the robbers in England had walked past his front lawn.

A bit grumpily I wandered off to find my pals. They were having a picnic lunch at our favourite spot, the bridge. When I found them and told them what I had seen, Sparky suggested we go back and have another look at Tom's cottage to see if he had returned. 'Or to pick up some clues,' I added eagerly.

Back at Tom's place there was still no sign of him or his grandchildren. We looked all over the cottage, and were just about to give up when Lump of all people found something.

'Hey, look at this!' he yelled from the kitchen.

'He must have found some food,' Sam laughed.

We went to see what Lump had discovered. Triumphantly he was holding up a piece of crumpled paper.

'Wow!!' Whizzer said sarcastically. 'What a find!'

'Look,' Lump said excitedly, ignoring Whizzer

and waving it in my direction. 'Read it!'

I flattened it out on the table to make it easier to read. It was just a letter to some shop in town, written by Tom, then crossed out.

'Good grief, Lump,' I complained. 'What's special about that?'

'On the back, on the back,' he protested.

I turned it over. On the back, in the same handwriting, was a list of dates and times, and at the bottom the words *caravan, surveyor, sheep, Staples*.

I couldn't make head nor tail of it!

'Don't you see?' Lump went on. 'Either Tom is involved in what's going on and this is a list of what he's been up to, or he is trying to find out what's going on, and these are "doodles" of the things that he's been thinking about.'

I was impressed. I was always underestimating Lump.

But it still didn't really help us. I just hoped Tom wasn't involved. I couldn't really believe it of him.

Then Lump had another idea.

'Caravan,' he said. 'I wonder . . .'

'Go on, go on,' I said.

'The men from that old caravan off the main road must have something to do with it,' he said. 'You know — where we stopped on the first day.'

Lump had more cause to remember the caravan and the men than anybody. I thought it was a bit of a long shot, but anything was worth a try! We had no other leads.

We sat down to think about what to do.

'Do you think Tom's in with these men?' Sam asked.

'No,' I replied firmly. 'But if we went to the police they would think so, on the evidence so far!'

'What do we do then?' Sparky asked. 'And shouldn't we tell Doug?'

Telling Doug didn't seem a good idea at this stage, but I promised Sparky that I would when we had something better to go on. We agreed to do a bit of quiet spying on the old caravan, keeping well out of trouble, if we possibly could!

By now we had begun to find our way round the area without getting lost. The main road back to the caravan led out of the village, up the hill, but in fact this road wound round the back of Staples farm, and so the caravan was only a few fields further on in a thick wood. We just had to cross the farm, and climb through the fields by a steep path to get to the wood.

As we walked along, carefully avoiding the farmhouse and Mr Staples, we spread out. I walked with Sparky.

'Lump does have some uses, doesn't he?' I joked.

Sparky was in one of his 'I've got to have a word with you' moods. Boy, friends can be really trying sometimes, especially when they are right.

'Look, Nick,' he said. 'You go on at other people because they say something about Whizzer, Raj and Chip to do with the colour of their skins, but you're as bad with Lump, just because he's, well, a little overweight.'

'A little overweight?' I choked. 'You mean fat.'

'You know what I mean,' Sparky went on. 'You treat people really badly. You were rotten to Sam

— and then there's Lump, and a whole list of other people. I heard Doug talk in one of his sermons about not being a hypocrite. You know, he was talking about what Jesus said about taking the plank out of your own eye before complaining about the splinter in somebody else's.'

'Yes,' I replied. 'Never did understand what he was talking about.'

'Oh, Nick,' Sparky went on. 'He *did* explain. The splinter is somebody else's little fault; the plank is your own big one!'

'Oh!' I replied. The light dawned!

'You can be a real hypocrite,' Sparky went on painfully. 'You're great at criticizing other people for the little things they do wrong, but lousy at noticing your own whopping great blunders.'

He was right again. I was just grateful that Sparky was a lot more patient with me than I was with anyone else, or with him. I don't know where I'd be without Doug and Sparky, but the message was getting through at last.

Why was I so dim?

We had nearly reached the wood where the caravan was.

'OK, everybody,' I said. 'We're nearly there, gather round.'

We had come round the back of the woods, so I told everyone to follow me and to be very quiet. It was a matter of crawling through the under- growth and Lump had to be restrained from calling out loud as branches, thorns, and thistles grabbed at him.

Soon we reached the caravan and crouched in the bushes a little way away. The two men were outside the caravan talking. The lorry was now missing.

Suddenly from behind me came a noise.

'TISHOO!!'

I had forgotten Chip's hay fever!

'What was that?' one of the men said sharply. They turned in our direction and began to walk towards us.

Now we were for it!

Then there was another noise, and the men just as suddenly turned back.

We all breathed a sigh of relief — very quietly!

Coming along the lane towards the caravan was the car belonging to Grabber's dad, and he was in it!

The men greeted him and must have told him about the noise they had heard.

'You're too jumpy,' he told them. 'Get in the car. We've got to pick up the lorry. Is everything secure here?'

They nodded their heads, climbed in the car and were off.

You could feel the relief among the gang as the car went away.

'What do we do now?' Chip asked nervously.

'We go and see what's in the caravan, of course,' I replied. 'Sam, Sparky, you come with me. The rest wait here, and if we get into trouble, run for help.'

When the three of us got to the caravan we carefully looked around to see if there was anybody about. Suddenly we heard a muffled noise from inside and jumped back.

I looked at the others and made a decision.

Reaching forward, I turned the handle and opened the door . . .

16

THE MYSTERY DEEPENS . . .

From inside the caravan I heard a noise.

'Mmmmm.'

I leaped back from the door and fell on top of Sam and Sparky who were close behind. We scrambled up and rushed back to cover.

'What on earth was that?' Sam asked.

'Dunno!' I replied.

We sat in the undergrowth in silence for a while. I could feel myself shaking inside with fright. I was so frightened I decided I just had to talk to God about all this. It's what Doug does a lot of — praying. It's funny, but the only time I find talking to God easy is when I'm in a mess!

In my mind I said to him, 'Look God, I've not exactly been getting things right, and I'm sorry for all the ways I let you down, but I could sure do with some help now to get this one sorted out.' I suddenly remembered the drama we had done in church. How Peter had denied Jesus three times, and Jesus still forgave him. That helped. If Jesus could forgive Peter, he could forgive me

Sparky was all set to give up and go back to the village to tell Doug. I could see all sorts of problems if we did that, so before anyone could agree with him, I summoned up all the courage I had and marched straight back to the caravan. I looked back to see a number of worried faces staring out from the undergrowth.

I gulped.

The door opened easily and again I heard the loud 'Mmm. Mmmm. Mmmmm!'

I stepped into the caravan and looked round. It was a grotty, dirty tip. Stepping over a pile of old clothes I went over to another door, to what I thought must be the bedroom. The noises were getting louder, coming from behind the door. By now the whole gang had plucked up courage and had come to the entrance of the caravan.

I opened the door and nearly died of shock when Ginger fell out onto the floor of the caravan. He was bound and gagged, and behind him I could see Mave and Tom in a similar state.

'What are you doing here?' I demanded.

'Mmmmm,' was Ginger's reply.

I undid his bindings and took the gag from his mouth. He fell back, taking in great breaths of air.

By now the others had come in to the caravan and were staring at Ginger in amazement.

'Get him outside while I see to the others,' I said to Sparky. Sam helped me to untie Tom and Mave, and then help them outside.

We started to fire questions at them, but all Tom could do was hold his hands up and say, 'In a bit,' between taking in gasps of fresh air. From somewhere Sam found some water and they drank it gratefully. I got very impatient waiting for them to get their breath and getting the feeling back into their legs and arms.

'Will you calm down,' Sam complained. 'And give them a chance? Just think what you would feel like after you had been trussed up like that!'

She was right, but when I get into something like this I hate having to wait. Patience is not one of my strong points, or as my mother often says to the point of ultimate boredom:

> 'Patience is a virtue,
> Possess it if you can,
> Seldom found in woman,
> But never in Nicholas Baker!'

Eventually, after what seemed like an age, Old Tom said, 'I suppose I had better explain what's going on.'

'Are you sure, Grandad?' Ginger put in. 'They look like a load of blabbers to me!'

I didn't like that. Nobody had ever called my gang 'blabbers' and got away with it!

'Look,' I responded fiercely. 'Nick and Co. never blab. If they did, they would be dealt with. Right?' I looked round at everyone and they nodded their heads in agreement.

Ginger didn't look convinced, but Tom went on anyway.

'Now come on, Ginger,' he said. 'They have tried to help, and they did come and rescue us.' Without waiting for any more comments from Ginger he told us what was happening.

Old Tom's story was long and complicated. We listened in amazement as he told us everything. Ginger and Mave's dad, Tom's son, was awaiting trial for a post office robbery which he didn't do. He had been framed by a gang led by Grabber's dad. Tom and his grandchildren had been trying to find some way of getting to the truth when they had stumbled into the sheep-stealing racket. But Tom didn't want to tell the police about what he had seen until he had got some evidence to clear his son of the robbery.

What's more, Tom's and Grabber's families had been involved together for many years in a little local poaching. When Tom was young he used to go poaching with Grabber's grandad and they were always trying to get him to join them again, but Tom had gone around breaking their traps. Now the two families hated each other.

'Ginger had been out looking at a badger set,' Tom went on, 'when he saw the lorry. He fetched us from my cottage. I rooted round and found my old camera to get some pictures to add to our other evidence. Trouble was, we got too near and they grabbed us, brought us here, and tied us up. I don't know what they're planning to do with us.'

The scene at Tom's house, together with all the other things we had seen since arriving in Tidesbourne began to make sense. 'It's all got very complicated,' Tom said sadly, shaking his head in despair.

'What was that surveyor, or estate agent, snooping round for?' I asked.

'Oh him!' Old Tom replied. 'Well, you see the sheep-stealing isn't the end of the story. Just recently I found out what they are really trying to do. They are trying to put Mr Staples out of business, as well as me. There are plans to build a huge housing estate on this land for people from the city. That would make our village what they call a dormitory town. If they get the land there would be no stopping the development and they would make tens of thousands of pounds.'

'Was that why your things were all thrown about when I first came to your house?' I asked.

'Yes,' Tom replied. 'They were trying to frighten me off my land.'

'Who's involved then?' I asked.

'Most of Grabber's family,' Ginger replied. 'The two men you have seen here are his uncles. Oh, and of course there's that bloke who works at Staples farm.'

'Frank!' I said. 'I knew it!'

'Yes, Frank!' Ginger continued. 'Another of Grabber's uncles!'

'What are we going to do now?' I asked of nobody in particular.

'I think we should tell the police,' Sparky put in.

'No!' Tom said fiercely. 'Not yet. I still want to try and clear my son's name. And I don't want you kids involved. It will be dangerous!'

'How can you stop us?' I responded quickly. 'We *are* involved!'

There was a long silence.

'All right,' he said eventually. 'But you must do exactly what I say, and not do anything on your own.'

Well I'd try. Actually, for once I agreed totally with Sparky. We should go to the police. But I could see Tom's point of view as well.

'To begin with, we have to find somewhere to hide,' Tom went on. 'They've gone off on another job, but it won't take that long.'

Then I had one of my ideas!

'I know just the place,' I said. 'Your wood! You know it so well that no one would be able to find you, and there's enough shelter.'

'Yes,' Ginger said. 'That's a good idea, Grandad. We could use the old gamekeeper's hut. Nobody ever goes there.'

We set off for Old Tom's wood with Ginger leading the way. When we got near the village we decided it would be best if the gang split up. So Sam, Sparky and I went with Old Tom, Ginger and Mave, and the others went back to the campsite.

We made it to the wood without being seen, and they took us to the gamekeeper's hut which was hidden deep within Old Tom's part of the wood. When we left them, I promised to come back with some food. We went out of the back of the wood and returned down the drive to the farm so that we didn't give the game away.

Back at the camp Sam, Sparky and I went to the kitchen tent to make some sandwiches. Things were running a bit low because it was nearly the end of our camp, but we managed to get together enough to feed them.

I had thought Doug was up at the farm talking to Mrs Staples and we would get away with it nicely. But suddenly and unexpectedly he stepped through the tent-flap.

'What's this then?' he asked. 'Off on a sneaky picnic?'

'Er, yes,' I replied, thankful for the ready-made excuse.

'No,' Sparky cut in. Then, turning to me, 'I'm not lying, not even for you!'

After that we had to tell Doug everything. As he listened his mouth dropped open.

'Are you *sure* about all this?' he asked disbelievingly.

'Come and talk to Tom if you don't believe us,' I countered.

He accepted my invitation and followed us into the wood and along to the gamekeeper's hut.

By this time the light was fading and it was getting dark. I was glad that Doug had brought his torch.

'Tom,' I called softly. There was no reply. I pushed the door open.

Tom, Ginger, and Mave weren't there.

They'd disappeared again.

17

ACTION!

Where had they gone? They couldn't just have vanished!

I looked anxiously at Doug. I couldn't quite make out what he was thinking.

We began to search around for signs of what might have happened to them. Suddenly I noticed Mave waving from behind some trees and putting her finger to her lips. She looked anxious and excited.

I told everyone to be quiet — then clapped my hands fiercely over Whizzer's mouth. As usual he had his Walkman on and didn't know how loud he was really speaking.

Signalling everybody to stand still, I went over to Mave. She said nothing but beckoned us to follow, and then put her finger to her lips again to make sure we kept quiet. I repeated her signals to the others and we followed in line through the trees.

After a short time, Mave turned and again signalled with her hands, this time to crouch down and stay still and quiet.

We were at the back of the wood. I noticed that Sam was taking the precaution of making Chip hold his nose, so that his explosive hay fever sneezes wouldn't give us away.

Mave parted some bushes very carefully and I looked through.

Straight ahead was the lorry — the one we had seen around the village and that had knocked Tom down, the same one we had seen by the caravan on that very first day.

Looking past the lorry, Mave pointed out Tom and Ginger hiding in some bushes. They waved to us and pointed further on.

In the field, and coming towards us, were five people, dragging along two very reluctant sheep. Even in the twilight I recognized them straight away — and I don't mean the sheep! It was the two men who had been in the caravan, Frank, Grabber and Grabber's dad!

Something had to be done!

We couldn't leave these men to get away.

I had my own ideas, and Doug and I had a whispered argument trying to sort out what to do. He could see that we couldn't just back off and leave, but Doug was also concerned that we didn't do anything stupid and dangerous.

We began to get everyone organized. Raj was sent off to get Mr Staples and the police, while the gang spread out to hide all round the lorry.

Chip had his own idea to do something and went round towards the front of the lorry.

'Trust me,' was the last thing he said over his shoulder as he crawled away. I hadn't a clue what he was up to.

By now, the men and the sheep had almost reached the lorry. I had to time the next bit dead right! I let them get to within a few metres of the lorry and then yelled as loud as I could.

'NOW!!' I screamed.

From all round the area, hidden in the under-growth, everyone began to scream, shout, and make as much noise as possible.

You should have seen the look on the faces of the sheep thieves. They nearly died of shock!

I suppose if I had thought about it for any length of time I might have realized how risky it all was, but things were happening so quickly there was no time to think. Fortunately for us, the thieves were so frightened that they didn't think it might be just a load of kids making a noise. They just panicked.

The sheep added to the confusion as they jumped about trying to escape, and it finished up like something from an old movie with everyone trying to go in different directions and finishing up falling over each other.

We just kept up the noise, with Tom and Ginger joining in.

'Get in the lorry,' Grabber's dad shouted. I had thought this might happen, but there wasn't a lot we could do. I hoped Raj had managed to get back to the farm and phone the police by now. But where were they? We needed them — *now*!

The thieves leaped into the lorry. Frank, who was driving, turned the key.

Nothing happened!

He kept trying to start the lorry, but it just wouldn't go! When I turned round, I saw Chip, a cheeky grin on his face, with his hands full of wires and things that he had removed from the engine.

Then came trouble. The men in the lorry saw

us. Angry because they had lost their sheep and furious because they couldn't get the lorry going, they got out and began to come towards me. One of the men from the caravan had picked up a spanner and was looking very menacing. I looked round and desperately tried to think of a way out. They were no more than five metres away when I heard the sound of a police siren.

Just at that moment Raj arrived with Mr Staples and Bill. The men and Grabber looked around and one of them shouted, 'Scatter!'

They all made off in different directions.

'Let's get 'em!' I yelled, and everybody got up and started leaping about.

The two men from the caravan were cornered by Mr Staples and Bill. Mr Staples had brought his shotgun and they didn't argue with him.

'Don't shoot, Guv,' one of them begged. 'We'll come quietly.'

I don't think Mr Staples would have fired it, but they didn't know that, and he sure looked mad enough to do it!

Frank was making a run for it towards the road. Sam saw him and was after him like lightning. She dived and floored him with a tackle that the Welsh Rugby Team would have been proud of.

Closely following her came Sparky and Chip, who dived onto him. Next came Mo and the final crushing blow for Frank was when Lump arrived. With a joyful whoop he jumped in the air and landed heavily on him. Luckily he didn't land on Chip and Sparky too.

'Get them off, get them off,' Frank pleaded, with what little breath he had left. It was obvious he was giving up the struggle.

Tom and Mave, together with Whizzer and Raj, had cornered Grabber's dad. He had looked threatening, but when the police arrived he gave up trying to get away.

That just left Grabber!

He had set off for the wood, with Ginger in pursuit. I thought Ginger might need a bit of help, and went off after them. It was a wild chase, as it was really dark in the wood. Grabber ran like someone possessed, not caring about the branches that snatched at him. I knew it must be hurting him, because it was painful for me too.

I managed to catch up with Ginger, who pointed for me to circle round and corner Grabber.

We eventually trapped him at the old game-keeper's hut. He stood there, his back to the wall of the hut, with one of us on either side of him. With a snarl on his face, Grabber raised his fists.

'Get out of the way, or I'll thump you both,' he snarled.

'Leave him to me,' Ginger said. 'I've waited a long time for this.'

Before I could do or say anything they were at it hammer and tongs. Now, I am the last person in the world to back away from a fight, but watching those two going at it I realized how stupid it all looked. I had to do something before Ginger knocked nine bells out of Grabber. He was like a lunatic. I guess there was a lot of anger pent up inside him, for everything that Grabber's family had done to Ginger's.

By the time I managed to separate them, Grabber was in no state to argue, and it wasn't too difficult to drag him back to the others, apart from stopping Ginger from setting about him again.

Back at the lorry, the police had started to push the criminals into the police cars. Then they took possession of a somewhat bedraggled Grabber. The car headlights cutting through the darkness made it look like something on TV.

Mr Staples took us all back to the farm, and his wife fed us and made us drinks. The police took statements from everybody until they were satisfied we had told them everything. This took ages and was very boring, but I knew from my dad how important it was to get everything on paper, and also not to tell lies or exaggerate. He had seen many criminals get off because a witness had exaggerated a story which made the evidence useless.

All the same, I was glad when the police eventually left.

The most pleasing thing was to see Mr Staples being so kind and apologetic to Old Tom, who for his part didn't seem to bear any grudges at all.

But the next best thing of all was falling into our sleeping-bags and getting a good, long sleep.

What a day!

18

THE WASP STRIKES BACK

The next day was our last full one in Tidesbourne.
Now it was nearly time to go home, I wanted to
stay. Funny, that! A few days before I had been
desperate to leave.

It was the day of the annual village fête — and
everybody from Tidesbourne would be there.
Honestly, all they seemed to do in this village was
have garden parties, sports, fêtes and all that sort
of thing — with lots of arguments in between!

In the morning I took the chance to have a last
walk round the farm. I left the others at the
campsite and set off on my own. After wandering
around the yard and talking to Bill, I strolled
around all the places that had become so familiar.

Together with the rest of the gang we also had a
last walk round the village. I hoped that all the
business over the housing estate could be stopped
now. It would be horrible to have such a lovely
place all built over. We all agreed that if they
wanted to build houses they should come to where
we live, knock down some of the old buildings in
the city that look such a mess, and build their nice
new houses there!

Back at the camp we started to pack up to make
the job easier the next morning. Lump helped me
take down the kitchen tent. He was a bit clumsy,

as it wasn't his sort of thing, but between us we got it packed into its huge canvas bag.

Only a week ago I would have been moaning at Lump at this stage, but I remembered what Doug had said to me in the boat. And Sparky's comments were fresh in my mind. It's very hard not to be a hypocrite, and very easy to notice other people's faults while at the same time quietly forgetting your own. Lump was a great pal really — he was just different from me.

The afternoon was great! There was even more food than at the garden party when we arrived, and the weather was absolutely boiling. The stalls and tables were all set out on the village green. We descended on the food like a plague of locusts, with Lump at the front.

Everybody was there. Even Georgina turned up and gave me a smile!

Before I could head off towards the food with the rest, Mr Staples caught my arm and pulled me to one side.

'I'm not very good with words,' he began. 'But I did want to tell you how grateful I am for all that you did. If I seemed a bit pig-headed it was because I was so worried.'

I shrugged my shoulders in embarrassment, blushed, and muttered, 'S'alright.' Well, what else could I say?

Fortunately, at that moment I noticed Tom, Ginger, and Mave appearing in the distance. They looked a bit nervous.

'I'll just go over to Tom and his grandchildren,' I said to Mr Staples. 'They look like they need some company.'

I hurried away, grateful for the opportunity to avoid what was becoming an embarrassing conversation. I think Mr Staples was quite pleased too!

'Come on over and have some food,' I said to the nervous threesome, but before we could get there Doug's dad, Mr Jones, started to make a speech. He was the chairman of the village council. He stood on a little platform with a microphone.

'Could you please be quiet,' he announced. 'And gather round.'

Everyone stopped what they were doing and walked over, except Lump, who kept eating.

'I'm not a one for long speeches,' he said — someone laughed, and Mrs Jones raised her eyebrows — 'but we as a village have a few thankyous to make, and one or two things to put right. When my son first suggested bringing his young people to the village for a holiday, one or two people weren't very keen. I think that we have all learned something from having them here, but most important of all, we have to thank them for saving our village from being ruined for ever by some very wicked people.'

Everybody clapped furiously, and we all blushed uncomfortably.

Mr Jones continued, 'I also have some tremendous news. Mr Staples has generously donated the use of his woodland area to the village council. We are going to make it into a conservation area, to be used for groups of people who perhaps wouldn't normally get the chance to come and observe the wildlife of the countryside.'

Everyone clapped enthusiastically!

'And also,' Mr Jones continued, 'Tom here has been offered, and has accepted, the position of unpaid warden to the reserve.'

The clapping was even louder.

Tom looked embarrassed, but happy.

Mr Jones' speech was over, so I joined the rest of the gang who were getting their food.

We were sitting around on the green eating, when I heard a car draw up. I looked round to see a police car, and out got the village bobby. Another man got out from the passenger side. He looked a bit scruffy and tired, and rather nervous.

'It's Dad, it's Dad,' yelled Mave and Ginger. They leapt to their feet and hurtled over to him. The tears were streaming down Mave's face. They nearly knocked him flat as they rushed over to him and hugged him. Tom followed on behind, trying to choke back the tears. He wasn't the only one, I can tell you! I even saw Mr Staples begin to blow his nose.

The policeman came over to Mr and Mrs Jones who were standing near us.

'Er, special session of the court this morning, charges dropped, that lot we captured confessed everything. Er, thought it might be nice to, er, get him home as quick as possible,' he said, shifting from foot to foot.

'That was a very kind thought,' Mrs Jones said, wiping her eyes. 'Come on over and have something to eat.'

'Don't mind if I do,' he said, and stomped over to the food.

We left Tom and his family alone for a bit, but eventually they came over and joined us. They were so happy. The change in Ginger and Mave was incredible — you couldn't shut them up!

It was a bit embarrassing really, because they kept saying how we had done all this and they didn't know how to stop thanking us.

Just then, I felt a hand on my shoulder. It was Doug.

'I want a word with you,' he said.

We walked away from the others and sat on the grass.

'I thought I told you to keep out of trouble and just enjoy a quiet holiday,' he went on. 'Sometimes I wish I had never met you — you're a walking advert for trouble! But I don't think that often!' He gave me a friendly punch.

I liked Doug. Even though he was a grown-up, he seemed to understand.

'You know, Doug,' I said, 'I've learnt a lot this holiday. When I get it right, life is a whole lot happier. The trouble is I keep forgetting and wanting to do things the Nick Baker way, getting in a mess, then remembering. Thanks for sticking with me.'

Doug just smiled and winked, and then walked away to talk to Old Tom.

I got up and went to join the lads at the village pond. They were sailing their paper plates across the water. We got really involved in seeing who could make the fastest boat, leaning out to give an extra push.

None of us noticed the drama developing just behind us. Now, you know how Lump feels about bees and wasps. Well, a wasp was in dispute with Lump over who should have the piece of cake on his plate. Eventually it decided to take action, and go for Lump — in the usual place!

That was how Lump came to be heading towards the pond — and us — at a speed which he couldn't control. He raced along, knocking us in like a row of skittles, then dived in himself to avoid a sting!

We all surfaced, spluttering and laughing. As we crawled out, starting to pick off the green slimy weed that covered a lot of the pond, Sam, Mo and Georgina came along.

'Men,' Georgina said, looking down at us, 'are such fools!'

That was too much for Sam, a loyal gang member. She may think we are idiots, and often tells us so. But she wasn't going to let Georgina get away with it, so she reached round Mo and pushed Georgina into the pond.

When Georgina surfaced, spluttering for air, all Sam said, with a smile on her face was, 'Sorry Georgina, I must have slipped!'

We all roared with laughter. Georgina did too, eventually. After we pulled her out.

The next morning we said our final goodbyes as quickly as possible and loaded ourselves into the old van. The journey back was quiet — no wasps, and definitely no caravans hidden in woods! It had been a really smashing holiday!

It was good to see Mum and Dad, and especially my dog, Wally. He licked me so hard he nearly took the skin off my face! Mum and Dad asked loads of questions.

'Did you have a good time?'

'Great.'

'What did you do?'

'Lots.'

'Did you behave yourself?'

'Yes.'

'Did anything exciting happen?'

'Not much, really.'

After all, it was all in a day's work for Nick and Co.!

More stories from LION PUBLISHING for you to enjoy:

Adventures

KILLER DOG	Peggy Burns	£1.50 ☐
NICK AND CO. IN A FIX	Bob Croson	£1.50 ☐
KATE AND THE MYSTERY PONIES	Sally Fielding	£1.50 ☐
THE INCREDIBLE WILL OF H. R. HEARTMAN	Jean Harmeling	£1.25 ☐
MYSTERY AT HAWKTOWERS	Chris Spencer	£1.50 ☐

Science Fiction

OPERATION TITAN	Dilwyn Horvat	£1.50 ☐
ASSAULT ON OMEGA FOUR	Dilwyn Horvat	£1.50 ☐
STARFORCE RED ALERT	Chris Spencer	£1.50 ☐

All Lion paperbacks are available from your local bookshop or newsagent, or can be ordered direct from the address below. Just tick the titles you want and fill in the form.

Name (Block letters) ....

Address ....

....

Write to Lion Publishing, Cash Sales Department, PO Box 11, Falmouth, Cornwall TR10 9EN, England.

Please enclose a cheque or postal order to the value of the cover price plus:

UK: 55p for the first book, 22p for the second book and 14p for each additional book ordered to a maximum charge of £1.75.

OVERSEAS: £1.25 for the first book plus 31p per copy for each additional book.

BFPO: 55p for the first book, 22p for the second book plus 14p per copy for the next seven books, thereafter 8p per book.

Lion Publishing reserves the right to show on covers and charge new retail prices which may differ from those previously advertised in the text or elsewhere, and to increase postal rates in accordance with the Post Office.